Purity is still a problem. Henry wishes he could get rid of the secret group trying to sabotage his business and the relationship between elements, but since they're a secret, he doesn't even know where to start. He has other things to focus on, though — his brother is still healing, he just lost his best friend, and he's in love with his bodyguard. All in all, his life is a mess.

Alcott has been Henry's bodyguard since Purity decided to target him and Edward. He's also been in love with him since then, but he knows better than to do anything about it. Henry already has too many things on his hands without adding Alcott's probably unrequited feelings to it.

But Alcott's feelings might not be as unrequited as he thought, which is a good thing. Henry's meddlesome grandfather, on the other hand, isn't, especially not when he tries to convince Henry's ex-fiancée to try to get back with Henry.

And of course, there's Purity, who's still threatening every element wielder who doesn't agree with them, and who might be closer than Henry and Alcott suspect.

Air and Earth
Copyright © 2020 Catherine Lievens
ISBN: 978-1-4874-2998-0
Cover art by Angela Waters

Published by eXtasy Books Inc or
Devine Destinies, an imprint of eXtasy Books Inc

Look for us online at:
www.eXtasybooks.com or www.devinedestinies.com

Air and Earth Elemental Unions 3

By

Catherine Lievens

CHAPTER ONE

Henry stayed strong until he left Edward's hospital room. Then his knees buckled, and he was flooded with pain, fear, and anger. He reached out, needing to hold himself up, but before he could touch the wall, Alcott was there. He took Henry by the arm and guided him toward the chairs that lined the wall. Henry was grateful, and he smiled at Alcott, but he didn't know if that smile was a real one or looked more like a grimace. He hoped Alcott would understand either way.

"I can't believe Lyle did that," he murmured.

"I'm sorry," Alcott murmured back. They looked at each other, Alcott standing over Henry, Henry sitting in the hard-plastic chair.

Henry didn't know what to do. He wanted to go find Lyle and make sure he paid for what he'd done to Edward.

He'd hurt Edward. He'd left him for dead. He would have killed Edward if Edward hadn't managed to escape. He needed to pay for that, but how? They couldn't go to the police and explain what had happened. Humans didn't know about element wielders, and it had to stay that way. What was going to happen to Lyle, then? Would he be released?

Henry wouldn't allow that to happen. He *couldn't*. "I want to talk to Lyle."

Alcott jerked back. "You can't."

"Why not?"

"You *shouldn't* see him. You already know what he did and why he did it. Why do you want to talk to him?"

"I just need to face him." Even though Henry knew Lyle had done it because he was with Purity, he needed more. Lyle had always been a friend, Henry's best friend. How could he have changed so much that he hadn't hesitated to attack Edward? Lyle and Edward weren't friends, not the way Lyle and Henry had been, but they'd been close. Why had Lyle attacked Edward? Why did he think elements should stick with each other? Edward had already explained that Lyle felt he deserved more than the job he had with the company, but Henry had a hard time believing that. He needed to ask Lyle, and hopefully, Lyle would answer.

But more than that, Henry wanted to get his hands on Lyle and hurt him the way he'd hurt Edward.

A hand on Henry's shoulder made him jerk. He looked up to see Alcott, his hands raised as if he was trying to make Henry see he wasn't going to hurt him. Henry realized he wasn't acting normally, and he tried to relax. Alcott was no doubt worried, and Henry didn't want him to be.

"I don't think it's a good idea," Alcott said slowly.

Henry shook his head. "I don't care. I need to talk to him."

"You have nothing to say to him, and I don't think he has anything to say to you."

Henry shook his head and rose to his feet. He felt better now, and he was thankful for the moment of reprieve, but he did need to see Lyle. "What would you do if your best friend did what Lyle did? If he attacked your brother, left him for dead? If he'd been working against you the entire time and you hadn't suspected?"

Alcott hesitated, and Henry knew he had him. They were friends, and Henry knew him better than he knew himself some days. He could tell how Alcott would react, what he was thinking about—how to keep Henry safe without stifling him. Alcott was quiet, and he'd done his best to stay just a bodyguard since he'd started working with Henry, but he was failing.

Henry couldn't say he minded. He needed a friend more than a bodyguard right now.

Alcott sighed. "Fine. I see what you mean. If my best friend did something like that, I would go find him, too. But you're not me, Henry. You don't *have* to see him. There's no reason for you to."

"I'd still like to, though. Please."

Alcott stared at Henry.

Henry held his breath. He'd found early on that if he said please, Alcott would be more inclined to do what he wanted. He didn't know why that was, and he didn't want to analyze it right now. He just knew that Alcott was weak when it came to politeness, and he was going to use it if he had to.

Alcott finally nodded. "Fine. Let me call the warehouse. I'll ask them to get him ready so you can see him. But it's the one and only time you do this, understood? I understand you want closure, but that's all this can be. You want answers from him, but you can't hurt him, no matter how much you wish to."

Henry nodded curtly. It was true that he wanted to hurt Lyle, but he knew better. He didn't know who was going to make Lyle pay, but he suspected Dakota wouldn't hesitate to take the situation in hand. If he didn't, well, Henry would find a way. He was going to avenge his brother, and he was going to find out who was behind Purity. Lyle had to know something.

He was done with anonymous notes, with people threatening him and his brother and his company for making good business deals. He was done with *all* of this. He didn't care who was behind Purity and what they wanted. They needed to leave him alone.

Alcott stepped away, but he didn't move far. He kept an eye on Henry as he took his phone out, and Henry stayed right where he was. Alcott was his bodyguard, and he always kept an eye on him. In the beginning, it had been irritating. Now, it was something else.

"What are you two up to?" Dakota asked, making Henry jump.

His heart raced, and he pressed a hand against it. "I didn't hear you," he explained when he noticed Dakota's bemused expression.

"I figured. Which means you're doing something you shouldn't be doing."

Henry straightened his back. Dakota wasn't his boss, and he couldn't make any kind of decision when it came to him. "I want to see Lyle, and Alcott is calling the place where he's being kept."

Dakota grimaced. "That's what I thought. I'd ask why you want to talk to him, but I understand. I'd want the same if he'd done what he did to me. Besides, he hurt Bay's mate, and that's enough for me."

"Do you know why he did it?"

Dakota arched a brow

Henry continued, "I know he said he felt he deserved a bigger role in the company, but that can't be right. He was my best friend, but he wasn't part of the family. Why should my father have given him part of the company?"

Dakota shook his head. "You know him better than I do. I can only tell you what he told Bay and me."

"That's why I want to talk to him. It doesn't make sense."

"If I had to guess, I'd say Purity probably set him against you. Even if he was only slightly resentful, they would have realized that, and they would have used it against him and you."

It made sense, no matter how little Henry liked it. Lyle had been his friend, but it was true that he was easily influenced. "I just can't believe he did this."

"I'm sorry for your loss. But you still have Edward, and you have us now, too."

Henry nodded, but it wasn't the same thing. He still had his brother, that much was true. Lyle had been his friend for years, though. It was like losing another piece of himself after already losing so much. Both his parents were dead, and the only family he had was Edward and their grandfather, who detested them. Lyle had been part of Henry's family, and now he wasn't anymore, and in the worst of ways.

"Everything is set," Alcott said as he came back. His gaze flicked to Dakota, but he turned his attention back to Henry. "We can go whenever you want."

"Now."

Alcott looked at Dakota again, and Dakota sighed and nodded. "You can take him. I'm going to hang around a little more to make sure everything's set here. Then I'll join you, unless you're already done and back home. Don't worry about me." He turned to Henry. "If you have any questions, feel free to call me. I'll answer if I can."

Henry nodded, but he was already focused on what was going to happen now. He didn't know what he would say to Lyle, or if he would try to hit him or hurt him. His life felt like it had imploded, and he didn't know how to deal with it.

"Are you okay?" Alcott asked as they walked away.

"I don't know. I don't know anything right now," Henry answered. If there was one person that he could be honest with when it came to this, it was Alcott.

Alcott was worried about Henry. He was always worried about Henry, which was his job, but he knew there was more to it. He couldn't think about that right now, though. Henry was about to face his best friend—former best friend—a man who had almost killed Henry's brother. If Alcott knew one thing about Henry, it was how much Edward meant to him. It wasn't going to end well, and Alcott didn't know what to do. He could have stopped it, made sure Henry never talked to Lyle, but he knew that wasn't possible. It wasn't because technically Henry was his boss right now. It was because he knew Henry would torture himself if he couldn't get answers. Hopefully, he would, but Alcott wouldn't put it past Lyle to string him along. If it meant he made it out of this alive, Lyle would do just about anything.

Alcott glanced at Henry, who was sitting next to him in the car. They were almost there, and Henry hadn't said a word since they'd left the hospital. He was probably still worried about Edward, and Alcott didn't blame him. Seeing Edward in the hospital bed had shaken him, too. He'd realized he was starting to care for the two brothers even before it happened, but what had happened to Edward had solidified that. Edward wasn't just a client. He was Bay's mate, and Bay was one of Alcott's best friends. That made Edward his family, and since Henry was his brother, it made him family, too.

Alcott shouldn't be as thrilled as he was by that.

"We're there," he murmured as he steered the car into the parking lot.

Henry leaned forward and looked at the warehouse. "It doesn't look like much," he commented.

That got a chuckle out of Alcott. "I realize that. It *is* something, though. It looks this way on purpose so that people won't realize what happens inside."

Edward looked at him. "And what happens inside?"

"I don't know what you're thinking, but it's probably not that. This is the place where Dakota trains us. He makes sure we know how to do our job. It's also the place where some of us live."

Henry blinked. "Do *you* live here?"

So far, Alcott had been staying in Henry's apartment. He

was Henry's bodyguard, and he had to keep close. "Yes. When I'm not on a job, I live here."

Henry wrinkled his nose, and Alcott had to look away. He didn't want to find Henry adorable. "Don't you want your own place, maybe an apartment? Isn't this crowded?"

"A bit, but it's what I need." Because Alcott didn't have a blood family, and these people, the people who lived there with him, who worked with him, were his family. He might not like all of them, but he'd become friends with most, and he was comfortable sharing a living space with them.

He parked in front of the warehouse and looked at Edward. "You don't have to do this," he repeated.

Henry's expression became serious again. "I *have* to do it."

Alcott sighed. "I had to try."

"I know, and I thank you for that. But I truly have to do this. I need to ask him why."

"You realize he probably won't have an answer for you."

"I know. I'll deal with that if it happens. I still need to face him. He almost killed my brother, and I will never forgive him for that."

"You don't have to forgive him. I hate that you're going through this, that you're losing someone you're so close to."

Henry shook his head. "I've already lost him. I just want to know why."

They exited the car, and Henry followed Alcott inside. Alcott had made sure everyone knew they were coming, so they didn't even have to stop on their way to Lyle's cell. Henry looked around curiously, but he didn't ask questions, and Alcott was grateful. He was tense. He didn't like what was happening, even though he knew he couldn't stop it. He didn't want Henry to get hurt even more. He had to protect him, because it was his job.

And because he loved him.

He nodded at the guard who was sitting in the small room

before the hallway where the cells were located, and Mercer nodded back. He didn't say anything, didn't try to talk to Alcott, and Alcott was relieved. The sooner they did this, the sooner they would be out of here, and that was what he wanted. He wanted to take Henry home to the apartment, to make sure he was okay, to make sure he rested and took time to grieve. No matter how angry Henry was, he was still losing a lot today. Lyle was his best friend, one of the few people he was close to.

Alcott wanted to get his hands on Lyle and strangle him himself for what he'd done.

Instead, he guided Henry to the cell Lyle was in. It wasn't hard to figure out which one it was, because Lyle was yelling, screaming at someone to let him out, telling anyone who'd listen that his lawyer was going to hear about this.

Alcott almost snorted. He managed to keep the sound in, but he didn't miss the amused glance Henry gave him. Then Henry shook his head and stopped in front of the cell, and Lyle suddenly shut up. He peered through the bars in the small window, and his eyes widened when he saw Henry there. "Henry. Thank God. You're here to get me out."

Henry took a step back. He looked outraged, but just like always, he took a moment to gather his thoughts, and when he spoke, his voice was cold and calm. "Take you out? Why should I do that?"

"You don't understand. I had nothing to do with what happened to Edward. I promise. I said those things because that man was threatening me, but you know I wouldn't hurt Edward."

"That's not what Edward said."

Lyle paled so much that Alcott wondered if he was about to faint. "Edward?"

"We found him. My brother is strong, stronger than you thought. He managed to get out of the place where you kept him, and he's in the hospital." Henry moved closer. "He's in the hospital because you hurt him."

Lyle loudly swallowed. "I'm sorry," he started.

Henry shook his head. "I don't care. Why did you hurt my brother? Why do you work for Purity? You never thought elements shouldn't mix."

Lyle hesitated, but he probably knew he wouldn't get out of it. Henry wanted answers, but he wouldn't compromise to get them.

"I was promised a higher spot in the company."

Henry blinked. "Higher spot? You already have one of the highest-paying jobs. What more did you want?" Henry paused, and his mouth slightly opened as he realized what was happening. "You want to be vice president. You want Edward's job."

"He doesn't want it anyway. You know he doesn't like to be vice president."

"I don't care what he likes or doesn't like. Being the vice president is his job, and it won't change. He's my brother."

"I'm your best friend."

Henry rushed toward the door and tried to hook a hand in between the bars and snatch Lyle.

Alcott had expected that, though, and he grabbed Henry's waist, pulling him back against his chest. "It's not worth it," he murmured in Henry's ear. "Don't hurt him. It's not worth it."

Henry wiggled. "It would be worth it to feel his blood on my hands."

This wasn't Henry talking. It was the pain, the fury, and Alcott knew Henry would be grateful that he hadn't let him do this. He held onto him, keeping him against his chest until he finally stopped moving. Then he held him some more.

Henry finally nodded. "I'm fine," he said.

"You're sure?"

"I'm sure."

Alcott let him go. Henry stepped closer, but Lyle had finally understood what was happening, and he wasn't close to the door anymore. Henry peeked inside. "Why?"

"I already told you why. Please, Henry. I know it was stupid. I know I shouldn't have done this. But I've been working for you and your father for so long. I deserved more than I got. I'm your best friend. I'm family."

Henry made a disgusted sound and shook his head. "As of now, you're *nothing*. I won't ever see you again. I don't care what you have to say to me or what you try to use as a bargaining chip. I don't care. You're dead to me, Lyle."

Henry turned around. He walked away, ignoring Lyle's screams and his begging, and Alcott followed him, not giving Lyle a second glance. As far as he was concerned, the man was dead to him, too.

Saying Henry was angry would be an understatement. He wanted to reach into the cell again, to wrap his hands around Lyle's throat, to tighten until Lyle stopped breathing. He was scaring himself with those thoughts, though, which was why he'd stepped away. No matter how angry he was, he wasn't going to allow Lyle to change him. He'd already changed Edward.

Henry knew what had happened would impact Edward for a long time, and he despised Lyle for it. He didn't want his brother to be afraid. He didn't want him to isolate himself. He wanted him to stay trusting the way he'd always been, and he didn't know if that would happen. At least Edward had Bay. They'd only recently discovered they were mates, but it was obvious they loved each other, and Henry was grateful for Bay's presence. He would do everything he could for his brother, but he knew he wouldn't be enough. Maybe he and

Bay would be if they worked together.

He had no idea where he was going, but he continued walking until he reached the door from which they'd entered the hallway. He could still hear Lyle, but he didn't turn around. He didn't care what Lyle had to say. He would never see him again, and whatever happened to him, it wasn't Henry's business, not anymore.

"Will Dakota take care of him?" he asked Alcott when Alcott reached him.

Alcott paused, then nodded. "He will if you want him to."

It was hard for Henry to imagine Dakota as a killer. Dakota was a nice man, and he and his mate, Benedict, had come to Henry and Edward's help when they needed it. They'd talked several times, and Dakota was a pleasant man, someone who worried about the people he loved, who wanted to keep them safe. "Will he do it himself?"

Alcott paused as he opened the door. He looked at Henry, then away. "I don't think so, no. We have people who take care of that."

It was a relief. "That's good."

Alcott blinked. "It is?"

"Of course it is."

"I would have thought you'd want Dakota to take care of this himself."

Henry hesitated. Part of him wanted that to happen because he trusted Dakota, but since he trusted him, he also trusted him to choose someone else to do this. "He doesn't strike me as the kind of man who would do something like that, and that's okay. He knows what he's doing. He'll choose the right person."

Alcott stared for a second, and Henry had to look away. He followed Alcott through the door. The guard was still there, and he looked at them when they came in. "How much blood do I have to clean up?" he asked.

11

Alcott shook his head. "No blood. We didn't even scratch him. Don't worry."

"Good. I don't like cleaning up blood."

Henry wanted to ask him if he had to do it often, but he knew better. Besides, he wanted to get out of here. He'd wanted to talk to Lyle, and he had. He didn't have a reason to be in this place anymore, and it made his skin crawl. He knew it was ridiculous, that it was only Lyle's presence that made him feel this way, but he couldn't help it.

A hand on the small of his back made him jerk, and he turned to see Alcott give him an apologetic glance.

"I think we should go home," Alcott murmured.

Henry agreed with that. "That's what I want to do. Unless you need to stop, since we're at your office?"

Alcott's smile was bemused. "We can go. It's not a problem."

"Are you sure? Do you want to grab something from your room?" Alcott had said he lived here when he wasn't with clients, and Henry didn't like the thought of having taken him away from his home. He liked the thought of being without Alcott even less, though, and he wasn't about to argue the fact that Alcott was still sticking with him. They might have stopped Lyle, but Purity was still a problem, and Henry suspected they would be a problem for a long time.

Alcott shook his head. "I don't need anything. I wasn't planning on coming back until the job with you is done."

Edward snorted. "It's probably going to be a while, knowing Purity."

"Well, we don't know a lot about them, but I agree with you."

Henry didn't care who they were or why they were doing this. He despised them, and he wanted them to stop. He wanted Edward to feel safe again, to be able to go back to his life, but he knew that with Purity still threatening them, it wouldn't be easy. They had to find out who Purity was, but where were they supposed to start?

"Did Dakota say if Lyle told him anything about who's behind all of this?"

"He'll tell you if anything happens, but I doubt Lyle will talk."

"I don't know. He sounded like he was willing to talk right now."

"Because he's a coward. He knows what's going to happen to him, and he wants to make it out alive. I doubt he will, though. Even if he knows something, he'll be dead if he tells us. Either way, this isn't going to end well for him."

"He might make a mistake." Henry hoped he would. But he knew Lyle, at least in part. His former best friend was shrewd, and he knew what he was doing. He might have panicked just now because he finally realized it wouldn't end well for him, but it didn't mean he was in a rush to die. Alcott was right. Lyle knew that either way, he would die, but he also had to know that Dakota would make it easy. Purity, on the other hand, would probably torture him.

Henry wanted him to hurt, but it was out of his hands. He didn't want anything to do with what would happen next. He didn't want the situation to change him, but it already had way too much.

He breathed easier once they were back in the car. He leaned the back of his head against the seat, closing his eyes and breathing in and out. It was over, at least for now. Lyle was in a cell, and soon he would be dead. Edward was in a hospital bed, but he was okay, and he would go home eventually. The situation with Purity was far from over, but Henry could relax, at least for a while. He could let Alcott take care of him, take him home.

He wished he were going home to someone. Jessica wasn't in his life anymore, though, and in a way, he was relieved.

She wouldn't have known what to do with the situation. She would have been horrified, and she probably would have cried. She would have freaked out, and Henry would have needed to pay attention to her and take care of her, and he would have done it, even though he would have needed something different.

But instead, he was the one being taken care of.

He didn't even care that he was vulnerable in front of Alcott. Alcott had been with him long enough that he'd already seen him at his worst when Jessica had broken up with him.

That was why he didn't protest when he felt the car stop—when Alcott turned the engine off and turned toward him. He didn't open his eyes. He was crying silently, the tears rolling down his cheeks, and he didn't jerk when one of Alcott's finger caught one. He stayed still, breathing in and out, but when Alcott took his hand, he squeezed back. He held it as if it were a lifeline, as if it were the only thing that kept him rooted in the moment. He breathed through the pain, through the tears, until he felt better.

He didn't know if he would ever feel better than he did now, but he knew that if it did happen, it would take time. He hated the entire situation, and he wanted to fix it. The problem was that he didn't know how.

Alcott's heart was breaking for Henry. He wanted to do more to help him. He wanted to protect him from what was happening, but he couldn't, not any more than he already was. He could protect Henry's body, but his mind and his heart were different.

He squeezed Henry's hand and waited. He knew he should ask Dakota to take him off the case and replace him with another bodyguard. He'd started caring for Henry almost from the beginning, from the first day he'd gone home with him to protect him. It hadn't gotten better. He still cared for Henry, and their friendship had blossomed. In Alcott's case, it had become more than friendship.

It was dangerous. It was hard to protect someone you loved, and that was the situation he was in. Because Alcott was in love with Henry, even though there didn't seem to be possibilities for him there. Henry had been engaged to a woman. Even if he was into men, this was the worst moment for Alcott to make his feelings known. Not only had Henry just broken up with his fiancée, but his life was in danger. It would push him into making decisions he wouldn't make normally. It would influence him, and Alcott didn't want that. If there ever would be anything between them, he wanted Henry to choose him because he wanted to, not because he felt like he didn't have a choice, because he was afraid of dying alone.

He wouldn't. Alcott would do everything he could to make sure nothing happened to Henry, and to Edward. Edward was in Bay's hands, and he was safe. After what had happened, Bay wouldn't stray far from Edward, not again. Alcott wouldn't want to be in the place of anyone who would go against Bay, but he was relieved his best friend would be there for Edward. He was happy for them, for the fact that they were mates, but knowing it reinforced the fact that Alcott was alone and in love with a man who didn't love him back.

It complicated things, but there was no way out of it. Alcott wouldn't leave Henry's safety in the hands of anyone else. He knew what he was doing. He knew his job. He could put aside the feelings he had for Henry long enough to protect him. Then, once he wasn't needed anymore, he might try to talk to Henry. They were friends, if nothing else, and he knew Henry wouldn't hurt him, even if he didn't love him back. He would be gentle in his let down, and while Alcott wasn't looking forward to that, at least he would know.

Henry was still crying, albeit not as hard as he had before, and Alcott hesitated. He didn't want to push Henry into something he didn't want, but he looked like he needed more, and there was no one else who could give it to him. Normally, Henry would go to his fiancée or his brother, but neither of them was available right now, and Alcott had to do something. It could backfire, but it could also be what Henry needed, and Alcott wanted to give him that. He wanted to be the one to take care of Henry, and when Henry didn't protest the fact that they were holding hands, he hoped that maybe Henry wouldn't be against more.

So he let Henry's hand go, ignored the way Henry's eyes popped open, and reached for him. He pulled Henry closer and wrapped his arms around him. Henry was tense for a moment, enough to make Alcott wonder if he'd made a huge mistake.

Then Henry relaxed, and Alcott did, too. Henry leaned against him, burying his face against Alcott's neck. Alcott shuddered, and he had to think about what Edward had been through to make sure that Henry wouldn't notice the way he was reacting. He wanted to comfort Henry, not to make him realize he was attracted to him. Now was the worst possible moment to make something like that known. Henry needed reassurance. He needed to know he was not alone, that he was safe. What he *didn't* need to know was that Alcott was in love with him and attracted to him.

"Thank you," Henry murmured.

Alcott didn't know what to say to that. He cleared his throat, because he wasn't sure he could speak, then answered, "You're welcome."

It made Henry huff a laugh, and Alcott supposed it was better than nothing. He waited, rubbing his hand up and down Henry's back, allowing him some time to gather his thoughts. Once he did, Henry straightened, and Alcott wanted to pull him back into his arms. He wanted to comfort him and to be there for him, but he couldn't, not that way. He and Henry were friends, nothing more.

Henry's eyes were red, and he rubbed them before smiling at Alcott. "Thank you," he repeated.

Alcott looked away. "There's no need to thank me. We're friends."

"You're right. We are. Still. Thank you for comforting me. I don't know what happened."

"You were overwhelmed. Your brother was hurt, and you lost your best friend, all in the same day. I'm surprised you didn't break down sooner."

Henry smiled deprecatingly. "I wanted to, but I had to keep it together. I couldn't allow anyone to see me this way."

"You allowed me."

"Because I trust you. I know you wouldn't use this against me."

The words made something in Alcott's heart settle, and it was one more piece in the love he felt for Henry. Since he couldn't do anything about it, he started the car again and drove. "Edward will be okay," he said for what felt like the hundredth time.

"I know. It's still hard, though. I want to be with him and to make sure he's fine."

"Bay will make sure he is."

"It's always been us against the world, you know? Even when our parents were alive, we were always close. It's hard to wrap my mind around the fact that I'm not the most important person in Edward's life anymore. He found his mate, and I'm happy for him. I'm going to miss him, though."

Alcott didn't fully understand that. He didn't have siblings, and most days, he was happy he didn't. Henry and Edward were extremely close, though, and it was easy to imagine how hard the situation was for Henry. "He'll always be your brother," he offered.

"I know. And now I have another brother. I can't say I ever thought this would happen, but I'm happy. Edward deserves this. He deserves someone who will love him and take care of him."

Alcott wanted to say that Henry deserved it, too, but he didn't. It would make him too vulnerable, come too close to exposing his secret, and he couldn't allow that to happen.

So instead he drove toward home. Henry's apartment wasn't truly his home, but it had kind of become so. It was a place he couldn't wait to go back to, both because it was easier to keep Henry in sight when they were there and because it was comfortable. Alcott liked living there. He liked how Henry had furnished the house. He didn't always enjoy staying with clients, but when he did, it made the work easier.

As soon as they were home, Henry made a beeline for the balcony. Alcott didn't try to stop him. It was where Henry went when he needed to think, and he liked taking care of the plants. He wielded earth, so it was natural for him.

Alcott made a quick sweep of the apartment, making sure no one had entered while they were away, before following him there. He watched him, sitting on the floor, with his hands in a pot of dirt. He was talking to the flowers, taking care of them, and it made Alcott's heart ache.

Henry was a caring person, even though most days he tried not to let it show. He probably thought that as a businessman, he couldn't. It made Alcott hurt for him, but he didn't say anything about it. It was Henry's life, and he was the only one who could decide how to act and what to do.

Alcott wondered what was next.

Lyle would be taken care of, and Edward was on the mend. They still had no idea who was behind Purity or what they wanted from the brothers. Now that they didn't have Lyle anymore, what would they do?

Alcott didn't know, but he didn't like the thought of anything happening to either of the brothers. The best way to make sure they were safe was to find out who was behind Purity and what they wanted—what they *truly* wanted. Alcott thought it had little to do with keeping the elements apart, and a lot to do with money and power.

He had no idea where to start, though, and he wasn't the only one.

CHAPTER TWO

Henry ignored everyone, making a beeline for his office. He barely stopped to smile at his secretary, who was staring at him as if she'd seen a ghost.

He supposed she had. People still thought he was dead, and he hadn't warned them that he wasn't and that he was coming back to work. They expected Edward, but instead, they got Henry, and everyone was staring.

Henry could admit he hadn't thought this through. He didn't like being stared at, especially in these circumstances. He couldn't ignore the fact that the reason he'd told everyone he was dead was that Purity had tried to kill him—and had almost succeeded. They'd pushed him into faking his death, and now, he had to deal with the consequences. He hoped people would eventually stop staring at him, but he knew it would take some time. He could already hear them outside his office, talking to each other, whispering and wondering what happened. He tried his best to ignore it and closed the office door behind himself and Alcott, only allowing himself to relax once he was out of sight. "That could have gone better," he muttered.

Alcott chuckled. "It also could have gone worse. At least no one tried to stop you for not belonging here."

Henry had to smile at that. "You think they would have?"

"Maybe, if they weren't so stunned to see you here. I have to say you made quite an entrance."

Henry looked around, but everything was as he'd left it. Edward had barely had the time to take his place as the CEO before he'd been kidnapped. "I didn't mean to. I just want to get to work and ignore everything else for a while." He knew it probably wasn't the best thing to do or the healthiest. He couldn't ignore the fact that Edward was still in the hospital, or that Purity was still out there, waiting for the right moment to strike. He wanted to, though, at least for a bit. He wanted to go back to his old life when he was just Henry, the CEO of the company.

It wasn't possible, but he could try.

It was weird to be back, especially with Lyle not being there. Edward's stay in the hospital made it even worse, but there was no way Henry could have stayed home today. Alcott had tried to convince him to do just that, but he hadn't pushed when Henry had told him he couldn't. Once again, Henry was grateful for his presence. He didn't know what he would do if he didn't have Alcott, and that realization made something squirm in his stomach. Henry pushed it away. He didn't have time for that. He didn't have time for anything that wasn't work.

He looked up, ready to go to his desk, when he realized Alcott was standing close, much closer than he'd realized while they were talking. He was so close that Henry could feel his warmth through their clothes, and he sucked in a breath, wondering what was happening.

Wondering why he didn't mind.

He took a step back, and Alcott smiled at him. Henry had no idea what was going on, yet at the same time, he did. It wasn't possible, though, was it?

He made his way behind his desk and sat in his chair, closing his eyes. He needed a moment, and he knew Alcott would make sure no one disturbed him.

What's going on? He and Alcott were friends. Henry was grateful he'd had Alcott by his side when he went to the hospital, then to see Lyle. He didn't know what he would have done otherwise. That was all there was to it, though, right?

He wasn't sure. He disliked admitting it, even to himself, but he didn't know what was going on with Alcott. He didn't know if he wanted something to happen with him. It was ridiculous. Henry had just ended a relationship that had lasted years, and now he was already thinking about the next person who could warm his sheets?

He tsked at himself. Of course not. That wasn't what he was doing. He didn't just want someone to warm his bed. He didn't want a rebound. He wanted someone to love him, someone who wouldn't care whether they were mates or not. He'd thought Jessica was that person, but she hadn't been, and while he missed her, he was also relieved that things had ended when they had. He could only imagine what would have happened if Jessica had wanted to check whether they were mates after the wedding, maybe after they had kids.

No. Ending things now had been for the best, even though Henry was sad. He also wasn't sure whether or not having a new relationship so soon was a good idea, but he couldn't deny that the thought of doing so with Alcott was both strange and intriguing.

He was bisexual. Not a lot of people knew it, because he hadn't had a lot of relationships. His last one, with Jessica, had lasted years. It had ended only recently, but he knew some people, like his grandfather, would start pushing women at him soon. He didn't want that to happen. He wanted to be the one to choose the next person he would love, and he was starting to suspect that maybe he already had.

Was it that hard to believe and to wrap his mind around? Was it that wrong that he already had feelings for Alcott?

He didn't know. He normally didn't care what people thought, but he couldn't help but wonder what *Edward* would think of it. Would he be happy for Henry? Or would he berate him for trying to find solace in someone else so soon after his relationship with Jessica had ended? Henry knew Edward would never judge him, but other people would. *Alcott* would, and Henry wasn't ready to face possible rejection and everything that would come with it. He wasn't ready to face a lot of things, especially with what was happening in his life. He wanted to tell Alcott about his feelings, to see if maybe they could have something, but he couldn't bring himself to do it, not yet, maybe not ever. At the very least, not until this thing with Purity was over.

He was still grateful for Alcott's presence, though, and even more so when he opened his eyes and found the man standing by the desk, looking at him. Alcott smiled softly, gently, and Henry couldn't *not* smile back. It was instinctive, and he didn't try to stop it. Whatever was happening, whatever Alcott was doing to him, it wasn't a bad thing. It was inconvenient, and maybe too soon, but not bad, and even though Henry didn't want to deal with it right now, he knew that eventually, he would have to.

He didn't want to lose Alcott. He didn't care if Alcott was his bodyguard or not, but they were friends, and he had very few of those, especially friends he trusted. With Lyle gone, the only people he trusted were his brother and the people who had come into his life with Dakota and Benedict, and that included Alcott. He was always there, right behind Henry, and Henry didn't want to do anything that might cause him to leave him.

"Everything okay?" Alcott asked.

Henry hoped his smile looked natural. Probably not. "I've been better."

Alcott looked around, his gaze stopping at the door for a moment, then moving back to Henry. "I can only imagine how hard this is for you, but we can go home if you want. You don't have to work here knowing that the last person in the office was Edward and that he was taken minutes after arriving."

Of course that was what Alcott was thinking about. Henry should have realized it. He couldn't know the turmoil going on in Henry's mind, and Henry didn't want him to find out. "It's not that."

Alcott arched a brow, clearly not believing Henry.

Henry gave him a self-deprecating smile. "All right. It's not *only* that. But yes, that's part of it. It's hard to imagine that Edward was taken from here, and even harder to remember what was done to him when he was and who took him."

"No one will take you. I'll make sure of that."

"I know." If there was one thing Henry was sure of, it was that. Alcott would protect him, whatever happened, whatever he had to do to make sure he was safe.

Alcott had to step away from Henry before he did something stupid like reach for him and kiss him. The instinct to do it was always there, but now wasn't the moment, and it certainly wasn't the place. Henry was here to work, and Alcott shouldn't distract him. There was already enough of that going on, what with Henry suddenly coming back from the dead, Edward being in the hospital, and Purity still at their heels, biding their time. If there was one thing he could give Henry, if he could give him peace of mind, then he would do just that.

He retreated to the small sitting area in the corner of the room, leaving Henry to do whatever it was he did. Alcott had never tried to understand. He'd been protecting Henry for several weeks, but all of that felt like it belonged to another world. Not that it mattered to him. What Henry did, his office, the people who worked for him—nothing mattered. What *did* matter was that Alcott had to stay close to make sure Henry was okay, and he was planning on doing just that.

He sat on one of the couches and looked at Henry, who had apparently pulled himself out of the mood he'd been in and had called in his secretary. She was staring at him with wide eyes, but since Alcott already knew she wouldn't hurt Henry, he didn't intervene. Unless someone he didn't know and hadn't checked came into the office, he would make himself invisible to Henry and everyone else.

He took his phone out. He'd learned in the beginning that he might as well read something while he was in the office. Henry seldom left, and when people came in, it was easy enough for Alcott to look up and check who it was. He didn't like being distracted, but he knew that waiting for eight hours, sitting on a couch, would be just as distracting as reading.

He unlocked his phone, then hesitated. He didn't want to read. He wasn't sure what he wanted to do, but since he knew Henry would want to check in on Edward, he texted Bay. Henry had called earlier, but something told Alcott that he would call again soon, and he could understand it. He wanted to find out what was happening through Bay rather than Edward, though. Edward was emotional, as was to be expected after what had happened to him. Alcott wanted facts.

How is he?

He didn't have to wait long for Bay to answer. *Good. Already chomping at the bit to go home.* Alcott had to smile at that. He wasn't surprised. He hadn't spent as much time with Edward as he had with Henry, but he'd been with him enough to get to know him. Edward liked being home, being in his safe place, and the hospital was anything but that. *What did the doctor say?*

They're considering sending him home later today.

You're not happy about it.

Of course not. I don't like seeing him like this. I don't like the idea of him being in pain, and I wish the doctors could do more.

They're doing everything they can. As long as he rests and takes his painkillers, he'll be okay. He had to be. Bay was Alcott's friend, and he'd just found his mate in Edward. Alcott didn't want him to lose that. He didn't want him to lose the man he loved.

Thinking about it made him hesitate. If there was one person who would understand what he was going through, it was Bay. He hadn't known Edward was his mate when he'd fallen in love with him. He'd only known Edward was a client, and he'd dealt with it, at least until he found out they belonged together. Alcott doubted that would be the case for him and Henry, but it didn't mean he couldn't ask for help. Bay would understand, and he wouldn't tell anyone.

How do you deal with protecting Edward while also being in love with him? he asked, regretting the words as soon as he'd sent them. It was too late to take them back, though. Bay had already read the text, and the three dots telling Alcott he was answering moved on the screen.

I wonder why you're asking that, Bay answered, adding a wink emoji at the end.

Alcott rolled his eyes. *Why do you think I'm asking that?*

I wouldn't know. Is there something you're not telling me?

Alcott hesitated. He knew Bay wouldn't say anything if he confessed and that he wouldn't think badly of him. He was going through the same thing. Still, it felt uncomfortably vulnerable to admit his feelings, even if it was to his best friend.

But he had to know.

Henry had just broken up with a woman he'd thought he would spend the rest of his life with. That and everything else told him it was the worst time to do anything, especially to mention his feelings. He wasn't planning to, at least not now, and that meant he had to learn to deal with the feelings and with the job, and he wasn't sure how. Bay's situation wasn't the same, not entirely, but he could help.

Fine. I'm in love with him. I don't know when it happened, but it did, and now I don't know what to do.

He sent the text and stared at the screen, wondering why Bay was taking so long to answer. The three dots moved, stopped, then moved again. Alcott glared, wondering what Bay was thinking about. Was he talking to Edward? Was he telling him what Alcott had just told him?

Panic gripped Alcott's stomach until he forced himself to think of the situation. Bay wouldn't say anything. Even though Edward was his mate, it wasn't his secret to tell, and he would never do something like that.

Alcott breathed easier, at least until another text arrived.

I can't say I expected this to happen, although I should probably have seen it when you started spending time with him.

That doesn't answer my question, Alcott answered. He understood what Bay was doing. He was taking time to think about it, so he wouldn't make a mistake when he answered. Alcott *needed* an answer, though.

He peeked at Henry before turning his attention back to the phone. Henry's head was buried in his computer as he did his thing, and he didn't even notice Alcott.

It's not easy, Bay finally answered.

You tell me. I'm already aware it's not easy. That's not what I was asking.

I don't know what to tell you. Like I said, it's not easy, and you're going to have to find a way to deal with the feelings and with protecting him. Did you tell him how you felt?

Alcott snorted, and from the corner of his eye, he saw Henry jerk. He smiled apologetically, and Henry smiled back, looking curious. Alcott couldn't tell him what was going on, so he shook his head, hoping Henry would understand.

He did. Of *course* he did. They fit so well together that it took everything Alcott had not to just blurt out the truth. Henry wouldn't thank him if he did that, though. It was too soon. Alcott turned his attention back to the phone. *I didn't tell him. I can't.*

Why? I mean, you're in love with him. You told me. Why not tell him?

How can I? Not only was his brother kidnapped and ended up in the hospital, but Purity is still coming after them, and there's also the fact that he just broke up with a woman he thought he was going to spend the rest of his life with. Do you really expect me to tell him I'm in love with him? Do you think it's the best moment to do it?

This time, too, Bay took his time answering. *I understand where you're coming from. You have to learn to deal with all of that, though. You can't put him in danger because of how you feel.*

That's why I asked for help.

Unfortunately, I can't do more. I can only tell you that with the way you're feeling, protecting Henry will always be your first and primary objective. It's not a bad thing. It's hard to push through the feelings when something happens, but hopefully, nothing will happen to Henry. It was hell when Edward was gone, and I don't know what I would have done if I hadn't found him.

Alcott didn't have an answer. He should have known. He'd hoped Bay would be able to tell him what to do, but instead, he was telling him how hard it would be to lose Henry. Alcott hadn't needed him to be aware of that, but he wasn't sure what to do with the information he already had and with what Bay had told him. He couldn't tell Henry he loved him, but would he be able to hide his feelings and to put them in the background while he made sure Henry stayed safe?

"It's lunchtime."

Henry blinked at the sound of Alcott's voice so close. "I'm sorry?"

Alcott smiled. It was a fond smile, a smile that made Henry want to lean against Alcott, maybe kiss him. Henry shook his head and focused on what Alcott was saying rather than on the feelings he created in Henry.

"I said, it's lunchtime. We should head out. Unless you want me to order something to eat here?"

It was tempting to say yes. "I do have a lot of work," he started, but from Alcott's expression, he knew that wouldn't go down well with him.

Alcott had insisted they have lunch out of the office every day since he'd arrived. He thought it wasn't a good thing for Henry to focus on his work so completely that he didn't even leave his desk for lunch. Henry couldn't say he blamed him. He found it easier to get back to work after lunch if he took a moment to distract himself, and lunch was the perfect moment to do that, especially when he ate with Alcott. Alcott had tried leaving Henry alone to eat in the beginning, but Henry had protested, and he was glad he had now. "I do have a lot of work," he insisted even though he knew it wouldn't work.

"And it can wait until you're fed and relaxed. Come on. We should hurry, if you want to get back to work soon."

Henry had nothing to say to that. He turned off his computer, relieved he would be able to look away from the screen for a bit. Then he followed Alcott out of the office. "You don't understand how much work I have," he grumbled without heat.

"I understand exactly how much work you have. I just don't care," Alcott answered.

That startled a chuckle out of Henry. "I don't think anyone has ever talked to me that way."

"Then someone has to start. I know how important your job is for you and the company. I might not understand it, but it doesn't mean I don't know. What's important to *me* is your health, though."

Henry arched a brow as they walked to the elevator. "My health? Does that mean you're protecting me from myself, too? Or that my computer was about to attack me?"

Alcott rolled his eyes.

He was beautiful like this, relaxed, joking around with Henry.

"I'm protecting you from yourself. It won't do you any good if you're too tired and hungry to move in a hurry if something happens."

Henry loathed that the conversation had gone back to that. "I don't want to think about this for a while."

The elevator doors opened, and they stepped in. Luckily, they were alone inside.

"Think about what?" Alcott asked as he pushed the button.

"Purity. The fact that they're probably watching me even now, waiting for the right moment to take me. I don't want to think about that, even though I know it won't go away if I don't. But just for a moment, for the lunch break, I want to focus on something else."

Alcott looked at Henry for so long that Henry felt the need to shuffle his feet. Instead, he stared straight ahead, looking at the elevator doors.

"We can do that," Alcott finally agreed. His voice sounded different, gentler, softer. It was a tone he didn't often use, and with no one except Henry, and it made something wriggle in Henry's stomach. It felt like butterflies, like when he'd started dating Jessica. It was ridiculous, but it was there, and Henry couldn't deny it, not to himself.

He couldn't help but smile. "Thank you. I know I can't ignore it forever, but I need a break."

"Understandable. Anyone would need a break in your situation. You don't have to think about Purity over lunch, all right?"

"Except if they attack me."

"Except if they attack you," Alcott agreed. "But if that happens, you'll be safe. I'm not leaving you on your own."

Henry wasn't surprised. Edward had been left on his own, and Lyle had used that opportunity to take him away. He'd abused his friendship with Edward, the fact that he was Henry's best friend, to lure Edward out of the office. Henry loathed him for that, and for so many other things. He understood why Alcott was planning on not letting him out of his sight, and he didn't mind. He might have in the beginning, but he couldn't deny he was afraid.

Edward had been taken, and he'd ended up in the hospital. It was partly Henry's fault for agreeing they should fake his death. He'd tried to convince Edward not to do it, but when he wanted to, Edward was incredibly stubborn. He'd insisted he could do this, and it had almost killed him. Henry would make sure nothing happened to his brother again, and if at all possible, that nothing would happen to him, either.

He and Alcott stepped out of the elevator and headed toward the wide front door. Henry nodded at the people they crossed path with, grimacing at the way most of them scurried out of the way. He wasn't a bad person, and he always tried to be fair, to listen to people, to be a normal person. Still, he was the CEO, and a lot of people viewed him like an evil person sitting on his throne at the top of the building looking down at them. It was ridiculous, but it was what it was.

At least Alcott, Edward, and their few friends knew who Henry really was. "Where are you taking me?" he asked as they stepped outside. It was sunny, and a gentle breeze ruffled Henry's hair. He briefly closed his eyes and tilted his face toward the sun with a sigh. He'd needed this, and he was grateful Alcott had pushed.

"I thought sushi?" Alcott asked, and there was hope in his voice.

Henry laughed. "Sushi it is. You can't live only on sushi, though."

"Watch me try."

Henry felt he'd been watching Alcott try to do just that since they'd met, but he didn't mind. He enjoyed sushi, and if that one little thing made Alcott happy, he was okay with eating at the sushi bar every day.

They could walk there, since it was only five minutes away, and Henry was relieved. He knew it made Alcott's work more complicated, but he doubted Purity would attempt anything in the middle of the street. Humans were all around them, walking and talking, barely paying attention to them, but they were still there, and Purity wouldn't want the humans to find out about element wielders. They weren't that crazy.

Hopefully.

Henry was still nervous, and he found himself wishing he'd stayed at the office. He knew he had to slow down, though, to make time for his personal life. Jessica had told him that several times when they were together, and they'd fought about it. She'd wanted him to give more responsibilities to Edward. He was Henry's brother, after all, and she hadn't seen a problem with that. Henry supposed it wouldn't have been one if Edward had been okay with it, but Edward didn't want more responsibilities. He liked his job, and he didn't want to change anything about it. Henry wasn't planning on asking him to, either. He wanted his brother to be comfortable. He wanted his brother to be happy. Besides, the moment Edward had had more responsibilities, the moment he had taken Henry's place, he'd been kidnapped and hurt. There was no way Henry was going to push him into anything.

But could see why Jessica had insisted he work less. He knew it wouldn't have saved their relationship. They'd broken up because Jessica couldn't live with the fact that they weren't mates, that her mate and his were still out there somewhere, and that one day, they might meet them. Henry thought it was ridiculous. There was no way to know if someone was your mate unless you tried mixing your elements, and it wasn't something one could do in the middle of the street or by mistake. He wasn't planning on doing that ever again. He didn't care whether or not the people he fell in love with weren't his mate. He just wanted to be loved and to love in return.

Of course, his gaze went to Alcott as he thought about that. What would it be like to be loved by him? Was it even possible? Henry knew Alcott pretty well by now, and Alcott wouldn't try anything with him, even if he shared his feelings. He was still careful, and he wouldn't want to push Henry. *No.* If Henry wanted anything to happen between them, he was going to have to be the one to take that step.

He wasn't sure he could.

Alcott had expected Henry to argue, and he had, but not as hard as he'd expected. He'd thought Henry would refuse to leave the office, and he'd been ready to fight him over that. It was Henry's first day back, but that didn't mean he had to spend his entire day on his computer. He could take a break, just like everyone else.

Henry was stubborn, especially when it came to his work and how much time he spent on it, but he'd given in easily enough. It was surprising, but also a relief.

That, and it made Alcott happy because he was going to have sushi again.

They strode down the street, walking so close to one another that their shoulders brushed together every so often. Alcott didn't move, holding his breath every time it happened, expecting Henry to say something or to step away. Instead, it was almost as if Henry was trying to touch Alcott on purpose, and Alcott didn't know what to do. Nothing, probably. It had to be by accident. There was no way Henry wanted anything more than what there was between them, which was friendship.

Alcott was relieved when they got to the sushi bar. They had a favorite table, and the people at the restaurant showed them to it as soon as they arrived. Henry might protest about Alcott always wanting sushi, but from the way the people here treated him, Alcott was pretty sure he was a regular client, even without Alcott. It was one more thing they had in common, and Alcott honestly had to stop thinking about those things. It didn't matter how many things he had in common with Henry. He was Henry's bodyguard, and he had to look at him that way and not as a possible lover. Alcott wasn't going to say anything about his feelings, not until Henry was ready, and he wasn't sure when or if that would happen. Certainly not anytime soon, not when Henry was still mourning the loss of his relationship and was worried about his brother.

They sat down, and Alcott looked around. He couldn't make a sweep of the restaurant like he would like to, which meant he had to be careful. He didn't see anyone who made him sit up, though. As far as he could see, everyone in the restaurant was either a worker or a regular. He knew almost all these people by sight, and with the way he placed himself, it would be easy enough to put himself between Henry and danger if something happened.

He hoped nothing would happen, though. He didn't like being interrupted when he ate.

Henry was quiet, and it wasn't like him. Of the two brothers, Edward was the quiet one. Henry was only quiet when he worked, but when he and Alcott were alone, or when they were with friends, he was chatty. Alcott didn't like how withdrawn he'd been since Edward had been taken, even though he understood why.

"I texted Bay," he said.

Henry's gaze jumped to his. "I forgot to call Edward and check in on him."

"Why don't you call him after lunch? I'm sure he's eating, too."

Henry shook his head. "I can't believe I forgot about him."

"You didn't forget about him. You were focused on your work. Besides, he's fine. I made sure to ask Bay."

Henry relaxed just a tiny bit. "Thank you. I should have checked in on him sooner."

"You already called him this morning. I'm sure he understands."

"Of course he does. He knows how dedicated I am to work. That doesn't mean I shouldn't check in on him, though."

Henry wouldn't stop beating himself up for forgetting about it, so Alcott stopped pushing. He wished he had continued when the next words that left Henry's mouth were, "Have you heard anything about Lyle?"

Alcott didn't want Henry to worry about Edward, but he wanted him to worry about Lyle even less. "I haven't. Do you want me to call Dakota and ask him?"

Henry hesitated. "Maybe? I don't care about him and what happens to him, but I do want to find out whether or not he's still in my life."

"As long as you don't want him there, he won't be in your life anymore."

Henry glared playfully. "You know what I mean. He's not in my life anymore, but he's still there, hovering. I need to know what happens to him and that he won't ever try to hurt my family or me again."

"I'll call Dakota after lunch."

Henry looked like he wanted to protest and ask Alcott to call now, but instead, he nodded. "Thank you. I know I shouldn't ask about these things. It's none of my business, not anymore. I just can't help but feel like I'm waiting for something to happen, and that Lyle might be the reason it happens. I want him out of my life forever, and that's only going to happen if he's locked up for the rest of his life."

That was certainly one way to deal with it, but Alcott didn't know if it was a solution Dakota would use.

This kind of situation was complicated. They were element wielders, and as such, they couldn't use the human justice system. Humans didn't know about them, and it had to stay that way. It meant they didn't know what to do with their criminals, though. They could lock them up, but since the elements were so separated, it might prove complicated. It was even more complicated to decide who was guilty and who wasn't, and Alcott was glad he wasn't in Dakota's place. He didn't want to have to deal with other people demanding things from him.

As far as he was concerned, Lyle was guilty, and he should pay for it. Whether that payment was his life or something else, he didn't care. He doubted Dakota would care, either, but he might want to keep Lyle around because of Purity. Lyle could be a way to find out more about the group, and it would be a pity to kill him before they had all the information they could get.

But Dakota wouldn't hesitate to get rid of Lyle. It sounded callous and horrible, but it was their life. They couldn't keep people in jail forever, not with the way things were organized right now. Dakota and his people, including Alcott, weren't the police. They were bodyguards, and they took care of their clients. They protected them, and if that meant they had to kill someone, then they did it. They had people specially trained for that, so Dakota or the bodyguards wouldn't have to take care of it, and Alcott was relieved. He didn't like the thought of killing people, even though it had happened a few times while he was protecting someone. That wasn't him, though. He was a protector, not a killer.

But if it came to it, he would kill someone without hesitation if it kept Henry safe.

Henry sighed and rubbed his forehead. "I apologize," he murmured.

Alcott wanted to reach over the table and take his hand, but he couldn't. Instead, he knocked their knees together under the table. "What are you apologizing for?"

"Everything. Asking so many questions. Putting you in danger. Needing you to protect me."

"You have nothing to apologize for. This is my job."

"Is that the only reason you're doing it? Because it's your job?"

Alcott sucked in a breath. He couldn't answer that question the way he wanted to, but he had to say something. "You're a friend. I'm not just a bodyguard, not anymore. I want you to be safe because I like you, Henry."

Henry stared, then finally nodded. "Thank you. I consider you a friend, too."

And if that was the only thing Henry could ever give Alcott, Alcott would learn to be happy with it.

He would have to.

CHAPTER THREE

When Henry sat at his desk, the letter was already there. He stared at it, wondering what it was, hoping it wasn't what he thought. He didn't usually get messages that were addressed to him in blocky letters. Besides, he'd seen this once before, and it hadn't ended well for him and his brother.

He peeked at Alcott. He was already sitting on the couch in the corner, his gaze on his phone. He looked up as if he could feel Henry was looking at him, and he flashed him a smile.

Henry forced himself to smile back.

He sucked in a breath. He didn't want Alcott to be worried or to start freaking out. That was what he would do if he knew about the letter. He would probably take Henry home and have a team go over the entire building—because there was only one way this letter had gotten here, and it was that someone had put it here, someone who worked in the building, who had access to Henry's office.

Henry swallowed. He wanted to open it alone. He wanted to know what was in there before telling anyone.

He looked at Alcott again. "Can you do me a favor?" he asked.

Alcott was on his feet right away, and Henry had to move some papers on his desk to hide the letter. "Of course."

"Can you go grab me a bottle of water?"

"I'm sure there are some in the fridge here."

"But the water in this fridge is flat. I'd like sparkling water. There are some in the kitchen on this floor. You won't have to go far." He knew Alcott wouldn't be happy about that.

After what had happened the last time someone had been left alone in the office, he wouldn't want to do the same with Henry. Henry could see the hesitation in his expression, and his smile softened. Alcott really cared about him, and not only as his bodyguard. He wanted to make him happy, but he also didn't want to risk losing him. "I'll be fine," Henry promised. "You'll only be gone for five minutes if even that. If it makes you feel better, leave the door open so everyone can see if something happens. I promise I won't leave with anyone, not even someone I know."

Alcott was still hesitant, but he nodded. "I'll be right back. Don't move."

Henry wasn't going anywhere. He watched Alcott leave the office, then, as soon as he was sure he wouldn't come back without the water, he took the letter. He opened it, not wanting to waste even one second.

He sucked in a breath. The signature made it obvious — it was from Purity. He had to force his gaze to move to the top of the letter so he could find out what they wanted.

We're not happy. You haven't listened to us, but we'll give you one more chance to make this right. Do what we want, and we'll leave your brother and you alone. Cancel all interactions with other elements. Cancel all contracts, all meetings, everything. We'll know if you don't do it, and we'll strike again. We won't limit ourselves to hurt your brother this time. We'll kill him and everyone you care for.

Purity.

Henry dropped the letter to the desk and leaned back in his seat. He wasn't surprised at what the message contained. He hadn't expected Purity to invite him over for tea. Still, it left a cold, hard feeling in his chest. What was he supposed to do? He didn't want to do what they wanted, but he had to keep his brother safe. That was the most important thing as far as he was concerned. Edward wouldn't be okay with being put aside, though. If Henry told him that he wanted to obey Purity's orders so he could keep him safe, Edward would say he was crazy and that he shouldn't even think about it.

And he wouldn't be wrong. Henry didn't know who was behind Purity or what they wanted exactly, but it was evident that if he gave in once, he would have to give in again and again after that. Once they got what they wanted, they wouldn't leave him alone. They would use him, and he would be their slave.

No. Obeying wasn't an option. How was he supposed to keep everyone he cared for safe, though?

Alcott stepped back into the office, and of course, he noticed right away that something was wrong. He almost dropped the bottle of water, but he managed to put it down on the desk. "What's wrong?"

Henry shook his head and pushed the letter closer to Alcott. Alcott's eyebrows rose high on his forehead as he took it, then he frowned. His frown deepened as he read the words, and he swore. "That's why you wanted me out of the office? To hide this from me?"

Henry shook his head. "I just wanted to read it on my own first."

"So you could decide whether or not you would do what they want from you."

"I have to keep Edward safe."

"He *is* safe. Bay won't let anything happen to him again."

"What if they hurt him, too?"

Alcott swore again, then, to Henry's surprise, sat on the other side of the desk. "Do you want to do what they're asking, then?"

Henry didn't know how to answer. "No." It didn't feel like it was enough, but what else could he say?

"But you're thinking about it."

"I just want to keep the people I care for safe. Is that too much to ask?"

"Of course not." Alcott's expression softened. "I'd do any-thing to keep you safe, so I understand. But we don't know who's behind Purity, and we can't be sure they'll stop here."

That was what Henry had been thinking, and he knew the answer to that. "They're going to ask for more if I say yes."

Alcott nodded curtly. "No doubt. Is that what you want?"

"Of course not. I don't want to be their slave. I want them to leave me alone."

"That won't happen," Alcott said, his voice soft and gentle. "I don't know why they fixated on you and your brother, but we already know they won't leave you alone. We still don't know why they left Benedict alone, but I suspect it's because they can't use him the way they can use you."

"Why? Why am I so different from Benedict?"

"The head of Purity could be someone close to you. It could be someone who hates you. We have no idea what's going on, and sneaking around will make it even harder to deal with. You can't give in, Henry. It's what they want, and we can't allow that to happen. We can't afford to be weak."

Henry tightened his hands into fists. "I know all of that," he snapped. He regretted his tone as soon as the words left his lips. He swallowed. "I'm sorry. This isn't your fault, and I shouldn't take it out on you. And I know that I can't give in to Purity. It will only give them what they need, which is someone who will do their bidding. They lost Lyle. I have no intention of replacing him. I have to make sure the company and Edward will be okay, though."

"They will be. I know I can't make promises, but I'm sure of it. You're not alone. You have me, and Bay, and of course, Dakota. We *can* make this work."

Henry wanted to believe it, but he wasn't sure he could.

Alcott was angry. He was angry at Purity for somehow finding a way to get the letter in. He was angry at Henry for pushing him away, for telling him to leave when he shouldn't have. He was angry at himself for doing what Henry wanted. The only reason he'd done it was that he cared for Henry, and that meant loving him was a mistake. It was the first mistake he'd made because of his feelings, and he shouldn't have. He couldn't trust himself with Henry's safety, not anymore. That much was obvious. Henry had needed him to stay away, and Alcott hadn't even thought twice about it. When Henry had asked him to leave, he had, even though it was against everything he'd been taught.

And now — he should be scolding Henry for doing it, but instead, he was trying to reassure him. It made him even angrier, both at himself and at Henry.

"I can't allow them to hurt my brother," Henry said, apparently not realizing the effect his behavior had on Alcott.

That was okay. Alcott would make sure he knew. He would tell him. "Your brother is fine. He's with Bay at the hospital. They won't let anything happen to him. You know that."

"I do, but what if Bay gets hurt? What if he's attacked and he can't defend Edward? I can't risk it."

They wouldn't solve anything by talking round and round the way they were. "The way I see it, you have two options. Either you give in to Purity's demands, or you don't. What will you do?"

Even though he understood where Henry was coming from, he prayed Henry would make the right choice. Giving in to Purity would be the worst thing he could do right now, or ever. If he truly wanted to protect Edward and the company, he had to stay strong and stand up to them. They would probably attack again, especially if he disobeyed, but there was no other way out of it. If he gave in, they would use him like a puppet, and it wouldn't be like him.

Henry's shoulders slumped as he sighed. "You're right. I can't give in. I hate this, though. I hate not being able to protect Edward. He's already hurt."

"You can't know for sure that they'll do what they say in the letter. They're using this to force you into something they know you don't want to do because they know it'll work. They're aware of how important Edward is to you. But even if you give in, you can't trust them not to threaten Edward again."

"You're right. I can't give in. My father, Edward, and I have worked too hard for his company. I can't give it away."

Now that they'd talked about it, Alcott had to tell Henry off for what he'd done. "You knew the letter was there when you sent me away," he said, his voice hard.

Henry seemed to realize he was in trouble. He looked away, sheepish. "I did. I saw it as soon as I sat down, and I wanted to read it alone."

He'd already mentioned that, but Alcott didn't understand. "Why?"

Henry hesitated. "I'm not sure. I guess I wanted to see what it was about before I made you freak out."

Alcott shook his head. "Don't you see? I'm already freaked out. Hell, I'm probably more freaked out than I would have been if I'd been here with you when you read it. What if something had been in it? What if it had been poisoned, if Purity had been trying to hurt you using that letter? What do you think I would have felt when I came back to your office to find you unconscious, or worse?"

Henry had the good sense of looking ashamed of himself. "I didn't think about that."

Alcott snorted. "Obviously."

Henry's expression hardened. "I didn't think about it, but I don't regret sending you away. I can promise you I won't do it again if that's what you want, but I had to do this on my own. Besides, Purity wouldn't poison me, not if they need me."

"They won't need you for much longer if you refuse to comply with their demands."

"So I won't open any more letters on my own. I'm sorry, Alcott. I realize it was the wrong thing to do, but I don't regret it, not entirely. And this way, I managed to have this conversation with you. I already know that if you'd been here when I opened it, you would have freaked out and whisked me home."

Alcott had half a mind to do just that. "It would be safer for you."

"Maybe. I realize that the fact that the letter was on my desk means that someone put it there, someone who works close enough with me that it's not weird to see them in my office. I can't run away, though. I'm not putting anyone else in danger."

Alcott knew he wouldn't get what he wanted, not in this situation. Henry was terrified something else would happen to Edward, and no matter how many times Alcott tried to reassure him, he wouldn't let that fear go. Alcott couldn't say he blamed him. He might not have a family, but he could too easily imagine how much it would hurt to lose Bay or Dakota or any of his other friends.

He swallowed. He had to do this the right way. He had to think of this the way a bodyguard would and of Henry as his client, not as the man he loved. "All right. We have to talk to Dakota about this. There's a mole in your office, one we didn't know about, and he'll want to investigate."

"I'm not happy about that."

"Tough shit. You don't have a say in this. You hired us, and we're going to do our job."

To Alcott's surprise, that caused Henry to smile. "I could

fire you."

Alcott suspected the smile he gave Henry was slightly feral, given the way Henry's eyes widened, but Henry didn't move away. He wasn't afraid. "You can try firing me, sure. But I don't need your money to keep you safe. I might be your bodyguard right now, but you're also my friend. If you decide to fire me, I'll just stick around as your friend, instead of both your friend and your bodyguard."

Henry didn't say anything for a second, then, to Alcott's relief, he smiled. "I'm not going to fire you or Dakota. I need you, and not just as a bodyguard. I don't know what I would do if I didn't have you with me right now."

It was a relief to hear those words. They made Alcott happy. Even if the only thing he could give Henry was love and protection, it was more than enough for him, at least for now. He didn't know how the situation would change once Purity was out of the picture, but something told him it was going to take a while for that to happen.

He sighed. "All right. But promise me not to do anything like this again. I have to know what's happening, even if you think I won't like it."

"I promise."

"What are you planning, then?"

Henry blinked as if he wasn't sure how to answer. "I'm not going to give in. That much, I'm sure of."

"Will you ignore the letter?"

"It's not like they gave me a way to answer. I'd tell them to fuck off if I could, but since I can't, ignoring it will be best. Since they have a spy in the office, they'll know I'm not complying." He grimaced. "I need to talk to Edward. I have to tell him what's happening and that he needs to be even more careful. We also probably should talk to Dakota. He'll have a better idea of what to do."

Alcott didn't know what to do, which was why he was just

a bodyguard and not the boss. "I'll call him."

Henry sighed heavily. "And I'll start packing. I doubt he'll want me to stick around, at least for today."

He wasn't wrong. Alcott was relieved. He wanted to take Henry away, to hide him from Purity. This way, he wouldn't have to fight with him to make sure he was safe.

Alcott made the phone calls. Henry listened as he called Dakota, Benedict, and Bay. Henry knew he should call Edward. He would freak out when he found out about this, and even more when he found out that Henry had sent Alcott away to read the letter on his own. He would have words for Henry, and Henry wasn't up to listening to them right now. *No.* Now, it was easier for him to obsess over Purity and what they would do if he didn't obey their orders.

Alcott was right. Even if Henry went along with them, there was no way for him to be sure they would do what they said. If threatening his brother worked once, it would work twice, three times. Purity would know, and they would use that against Henry. Every time they wanted something from him, they would threaten Edward.

And Henry would give in. Edward was his only family. Their grandfather was still alive, but they'd never gotten along with him, and Henry was pretty sure he didn't like them. They didn't see him often, and that was on purpose. Henry wasn't planning on changing that, but it did mean Edward only had him.

Well, he had him, Bay, Alcott, Dakota, and Benedict now.

Henry sucked in a breath. They weren't alone facing this. They would have been a few months ago, but that had changed. He had to have faith in everyone. He had to trust they knew what they were doing, how to do their jobs. It was hard to leave that kind of decision in someone else's hands, but it was the only thing Henry could do. He'd already shown he didn't think clearly when it came to Purity.

Dakota would know what to do. He and Benedict had more experience with Purity than Henry. They would be able to help, and that was all Henry wanted. Well, he wanted Purity out of his life, but he doubted that would happen. In the meantime, this was better than nothing.

Alcott finally hung up. "They'll meet us at your brother's apartment."

Henry frowned. "Isn't it too soon for him to leave the hospital?"

Alcott snorted. "It's a small miracle he stayed there as long as he did. You know he was going crazy."

Henry did. He visited Edward every day, and he'd insisted the doctors keep him longer than necessary. It was for his own peace of mind, but obviously, that was over now. It wasn't a bad thing. With everything that was happening, he was starting to realize that he was treating Edward like a child. His need to keep his brother safe was making him act in a way he shouldn't, and Edward would eventually realize that if he hadn't already. Then he would tear Henry a new one. Edward was quiet, but that didn't mean he didn't speak up for himself when he had to.

Besides, Edward had Bay now. Henry shouldn't be the one to make decisions about him, not anymore. It would take time to wrap his mind around that and get used to it, but he could do it.

He had to.

"When did he go home?" He hadn't called Edward since earlier that morning, and Edward hadn't called him. He'd been at the hospital last night, though. Hopefully, he hadn't found out Henry had talked to his doctor. Henry couldn't find it in himself to feel guilty about it. Edward wouldn't be happy, but at least Henry had managed to have a few days in which he wasn't terrified Edward would be attacked.

"Today. I'm surprised he hasn't called you yet."

Henry shrugged. "He's probably going to do it at any moment." And Henry wasn't looking forward to it. He didn't want to give his brother the news that Purity was demanding this of him. He didn't want Edward to know that he'd been tempted to say yes for his sake. Edward would be angry, and he wouldn't let Henry hear the end of it.

But Henry wouldn't give in. No matter how much he wanted to, no matter how much he wanted to keep Edward safe, he couldn't make that kind of decision, not on his own. It was fear talking, and that he shouldn't listen to it.

"He's okay," Alcott murmured.

"I know he is. He's with Bay."

Alcott's smile widened. "He is, and Bay loves him. He won't let anything happen to him, Purity or not. You can trust Bay. Edward's his mate. Bay would die to protect him."

Henry grimaced. "Let's hope it doesn't come to that because Edward would be a mess if it happened."

"He would be, but he wouldn't be alone. He has you and all of us. We're not going anywhere, Henry. You have to understand and accept that. I know you're used to facing all of this on your own, but you don't have to anymore."

It was a habit. Henry was so used to dealing with everything on his own that it was instinct for him. He even tried to keep Edward away from some of the decisions, knowing Edward didn't want that kind of power in the company. This didn't have anything to do with the company, though, not really. It had to do with power, but what Purity was trying to do—with what they were trying to force Henry's hand to do. He couldn't keep that a secret from Edward.

He rose from his chair. "We should probably go."

Alcott mirrored his movement, getting to his feet. "You're right. The sooner we head out, the sooner this will be over.

You think you'll want to come back to work once the meeting is over?"

Henry looked around. His first instinct was to say yes, but he didn't. "I think I'll head home."

Alcott nodded. "I'm surprised but relieved."

"I don't think I'll be able to work here, not knowing that someone I trust and work with every day is part of Purity." He'd already been through that once with Lyle, and he wasn't ready to face that kind of thing again.

"I know it's hard, especially after what happened with Lyle. I can't promise you everything will be okay, but I can promise that I'll keep you safe and that I won't ever betray you."

Henry knew it was true. He wasn't sure why he was so convinced of it, but it didn't matter.

He gathered his things, put them in his bag, and together, they headed toward the door. He let Alcott take the lead, just like always. It was important for Alcott to make sure that wherever they were going, the place was safe. It was his job, but there was more to it. Like Alcott had said many times, the two of them were friends. Henry didn't know what he would be doing right now if he didn't have Alcott. He would go crazy, probably.

And he wanted more. He couldn't bring it up, not now, maybe not until Purity was dealt with, but he was starting to hate the distance between him and Alcott. They were friends, yes. That was all they were, at least for now, but he needed more. He needed to feel someone against him, someone holding him, someone reassuring him and comforting him that everything would be okay. He needed to be hugged, to be held. He knew it was the situation causing that, and he probably wouldn't feel that way if Purity hadn't sent him the letter—or maybe he would. He didn't know. Spending time with Alcott seemed to bring out a softer part of himself, a part he seldom allowed to surface. He couldn't be vulnerable and weak, not when he was guiding the company.

But maybe with Alcott he could. With him, he *wanted* to be vulnerable, to allow Alcott to see who he really was. He didn't know if it was possible, though, and he was afraid to hope.

Alcott drove them to Edward's apartment. Henry was quiet in the passenger seat—too quiet. Alcott wanted him to speak, to tell him what he was feeling, but he didn't ask. Henry wasn't usually as quiet as Edward, but this situation was far from normal. He no doubt wanted some time to wrap his mind around what had just happened. He had conflicting feelings about it like anyone would.

Alcott knew Henry wanted to give in to Purity to keep his brother safe, but there was no way to know whether or not they would keep their promise of leaving them alone after that. Henry knew that, but his first instinct was to ignore it and give in. Alcott was relieved he wasn't planning to, but he knew all too well that people changed their minds—that they made decisions they shouldn't make. He hoped talking with Edward would help, but he wasn't convinced. Henry was freaking out about his brother, and seeing how injured he was wouldn't help. Still, there was no way out of this. They had to have this meeting, and that meant putting Henry and Edward in the same room and having them talk about the letter.

Alcott wasn't stupid, and neither was Edward. They both knew what Henry had done with the doctor, even though Edward hadn't said anything. Alcott hadn't, either, because it wasn't his business, but he didn't understand why Edward hadn't protested. Maybe he understood how important it was for Henry. Maybe he'd truly needed more days to rest and heal. Whatever the reason, that was something between the brothers and not Alcott's business. He couldn't make it his.

The silence in the car was heavy, and it only grew heavier as they neared Edward's apartment. Alcott wished they could go back in time, to before Edward had been hurt. It wasn't merely the company that was threatened. It was Henry's brother, the most important person in his life. Henry wanted to keep Edward safe, but he didn't know how to do it.

Alcott parked in the garage under the building. They both stayed still for a moment as the engine ticked away. Then, Alcott reached for the door. Henry knew what to do. He had to wait in the car until Alcott was sure the garage was safe. It should be, but Alcott wouldn't risk it, especially not after the letter. He wouldn't put it past Purity to try to force Henry's hand, and he wouldn't let that happen.

He couldn't.

He'd never wanted to wrap his arms around Henry more than he did now. He wanted to be there for him as more than a friend, to support him, to help him make the decisions he had to make. The fact that he couldn't hurt him, but he realized that now was the worst moment to dump his feelings on Henry. Henry had to focus on Edward and the company, on keeping everyone he loved safe. It wouldn't help if Alcott told him he loved him and Henry didn't share his feelings. Then they would lose each other, and Alcott wouldn't be able to be there for Henry.

He had to keep his mouth shut. He had to keep his feelings to himself. Henry's life was already a mess. He didn't need to make it even more so.

He nodded, and Henry slipped out of the car. Together, they headed to the elevator, Alcott looking around as if he expected someone to jump from behind one of the cars. Again, he wouldn't put it past Purity to do something like that.

They made it to the apartment safe and in one piece, though. The door flew open, and Bay stood there, waiting. He looked the same as usual, yet different. He was more relaxed than the last time Alcott had seen him at the hospital, but there were still lines of tension around his eyes and mouth. He still smiled as he gestured at them to enter. "He's in the living room. Benedict and Dakota are, too. You're the last ones to arrive."

"I apologize," Henry said, his voice painfully cold. "I had to finish what I was doing at the office."

Bay blinked at him. "I wasn't blaming you. I was just telling you that you're the last one to arrive."

Henry cleared his throat. "I'm sorry."

"Don't apologize. I know you're tense. I don't blame you for it, either. You want something to drink before we get to this?"

Henry shook his head. "I just want to get to the bottom of it and forget about it."

Bay snorted. "Something tells me that's not going to be as easy as you."

He led them to the living room, even though they knew where it was. Edward was sitting on the couch, his back against a mountain of pillows, his lower body tightly wrapped in a blanket. He looked exasperated but fond as he looked at Bay. Those two loved each other, and the sight of it made something ache in Alcott's chest. He loved Henry, but he couldn't have him. It wasn't fair, but then when was life fair? He didn't even know if Henry shared his feelings.

Dakota opened his hand, and Henry didn't have to ask what he wanted. He took the letter from his bag, dumped the bag on one of the armchairs, and put the letter in Dakota's hand. He and Benedict, with Bay right behind them, leaned over to read.

Edward looked like he wanted to do the same, but one glare from Bay made sure he wouldn't move from the couch. He huffed, then turned his attention to his brother. "How are you feeling?"

Alcott didn't belong with either group. He wasn't a sibling, and he'd already read the letter. So he hovered awkwardly until Bay finally realized what was happening and pointed him to an armchair. "Sit down. You're making me nervous standing there."

Alcott rolled his eyes, but he obeyed, relieved. Henry and Edward were sitting next to each other, already whispering, and he kept an eye on them until everyone else was done reading the letter.

"There's a spy in your office," Benedict said.

Henry nodded. "There is. There's no other way for Purity to get a letter on my desk."

"What does the letter say?" Edward asked. He glared at Henry. "And don't try to feed me some bullshit. I'm going to read it whether you like it or not."

Henry tensed, then relaxed. "They want me to sever all contacts both me and the company have with other elements. They want me to cancel contracts and stay away. If I do it, they won't touch you again. You'll be safe."

Edward made a strangled sound. "You don't believe them, do you? Because they won't do anything of the sort. They're playing you, Henry." When Henry didn't say anything, Edward grabbed one of his hands. "Please, tell me you're not thinking about doing this."

Henry finally shook his head. "I know we can't trust them. I know that if I give in this time, they'll continue using me. I'm afraid of losing you, though."

"You won't."

"You can't promise that. Look at you. You're hurt. You just spent a week in the hospital."

"Only because you convinced the doctor to keep me there for a week. I didn't *need* to be there for a week, Henry. I'm fine. The only reason I'm not moving is that Bay will kill me if I try to get up. He's almost as bad as you are, coddling me as if I were a baby. But I promise I'm feeling fine, and I don't want you to get involved with Purity, not after what they did to me. It's not only that you can't trust them. They already attacked me. Do you think you can work with someone who did that to me?"

They all knew the answer to that.

Henry shook his head and looked around. "I won't give in. They're going to do something if I don't, though. None of us is safe."

"We have to find out who's behind Purity," Dakota said.

They looked at each other. They had no idea where to start, and the letter wasn't helping. There was a hint of desperation in Dakota's voice, and they all knew what he was thinking.

They had to find who was behind Purity before something happened to Henry and Edward.

Chapter Four

Henry couldn't seem to settle down. He'd tried relaxing, since it was Saturday and Edward had forbidden him to go to work, but he couldn't. His thoughts kept going to the letter he'd gotten from Purity, to the fear of losing his brother, to not knowing what was happening. He loathed not knowing. He didn't like not having all the tools he needed to defeat Purity.

The main problem was that they still didn't know who Purity was. Dakota and Benedict suspected there was one man behind it and that he was the cause for everything, and Henry tended to agree. It was obviously someone who knew the three of them pretty well, too. There was no other way for Purity to know what kind of business deals they signed. That meant the Purity leader was probably a CEO or someone who worked either for Benedict or for Edward and Henry.

That didn't help as much as it should. It could be someone who worked for them, but it could also be someone who worked at another company. They'd gone over names, but they hadn't settled on any of them, and it made Henry antsy. He wanted to do something. Having to sit at home, waiting, made his stomach churn. He was tempted to ignore Edward's words and head to the office, but he knew better. His brother would have his ass if he did. He'd insisted Henry needed rest as much as he did, even though Henry hadn't been wounded, and Henry had given in to make Edward happy. Now, he kind of regretted it.

He was sitting on the balcony, his hands in a pot of dirt.

There was nothing to do with his plants and flowers, though. Lately, he'd been so stressed that he'd been taking extra care of them. They were watered and happy, and while usually sitting there with them was enough for Henry to feel better, it wasn't working this time.

He huffed and took his hands out of the pot, brushing them against his jeans. They were old clothes, things he didn't wear to work, so he didn't care if they got dirty. He got to his feet, enjoying the warmth of the tiles under his bare feet, and stretched.

"You have to stay still for a bit," Alcott murmured.

Henry turned to look at him. He was stretched out in one of the chairs Henry kept on the balcony, his eyes half-closed as he basked in the sun. He reminded Henry of a big cat, and it made Henry smile. Not that there was a lot to smile about, considering everything. It helped to have Alcott close, though.

"I don't know what to do," Henry confessed.

Alcott opened his eyes and straightened in the armchair. "Do you want to go out?"

That made Henry smile, too. "I know you don't want me to go out."

Alcott chuckled. "You're right. I want you to stay home. I don't want you to put yourself in danger. I know better than to ask you to stay here if you don't want to, though."

Henry was tempted to say yes. He didn't have to go to work. He and Alcott could do something else, maybe grab dinner later or watch a movie.

But no. Alcott couldn't get distracted, not after the letter. He had to be focused on Henry's safety, and that would be easier to do if they stayed home. Henry didn't like it, but he would like it even less if they got hurt, or worse, killed. "We'll stay in," he decided.

"Are you sure?"

"I'm sure. Start thinking about what you want for dinner, though."

The corners of Alcott's lips curled. "Are you offering to cook for me?"

"I would if I wanted to kill you."

That made Alcott laugh, and Henry relaxed even more. He loved that sound, and he thought Alcott didn't smile enough. He probably didn't have a reason to, considering the situation, but hearing him made Henry feel better.

"I'm not cooking," Alcott said.

"I never said you were cooking. I was thinking of takeout."

Alcott rose from his chair and stretched like Henry had done just minutes earlier. Henry couldn't look away. He hoped Alcott wouldn't mind if he caught him staring, but then, how could he look away? Alcott was a work of art. His body was long and slim, but Henry could see the muscles bunch under his skin. He was wearing jeans and a t-shirt, looking more like he was having fun with Henry rather than like he was his bodyguard. Henry knew he was lethal, though, and he was grateful for his presence. He was grateful for his friendship, too, even though he found himself excited at the thought of having more with him.

Maybe now was the right moment to bring it up. They would be stuck in the apartment for two days, and they would have time to talk things out. What would happen if Alcott didn't want Henry, though? Would he still be comfortable being his bodyguard? Henry didn't know, and he wasn't sure he could risk both that and his friendship with Alcott.

He sighed. "I'm hungry."

Alcott blinked at him. "Already? We only had breakfast an hour ago."

"Being bored makes me hungry."

"It's more like boredom makes you eat, but fine. Let's go inside and find something to eat."

They headed to the kitchen. Henry *wasn't* hungry, but he was bored, and eating would help, at least for a bit. It wasn't a habit he wanted to get into, but he was only stuck here for two days. Surely he could relax his rules a bit?

"What did you have in mind?" Alcott asked as he opened the fridge.

"Is there any fruit in there?"

"You have strawberries, bananas, and I'm pretty sure I saw an apple or two in that bowl on the counter."

"How about a fruit salad?"

Alcott turned to look at Henry, nodding. "Sounds good. Start with the apples. I'm taking care of the rest."

They worked side by side, and it was comfortable. It was *familiar*, something Henry wasn't used to. The only person who had come to his house regularly before all of this happened was Edward — and Lyle, but Henry didn't want to think about him. Henry wasn't happy about the situation and what had brought him and the others together, but he couldn't deny this was a perk. He wasn't alone anymore.

Jessica had come regularly, too, and while they'd loved each other, their relationship had been different. They didn't have quiet moments like the one Henry was having with Alcott. Jessica always wanted to talk, to plan things. She was a planner, and she didn't like doing things without knowing what would happen next. Henry was like that usually, too, at least when it came to his work. In his private life, though, he liked being surprised, and that wasn't something Jessica had understood.

Alcott suddenly tensed next to Henry, and Henry almost dropped his knife. He looked at Alcott, who turned to face the kitchen door. "Are we expecting someone?"

Henry blinked. "What you mean?"

"Someone is unlocking the door."

Fear gripped Henry's throat before he could remember

that only a few people had a key. "It's probably Edward."

"I don't think so. Bay would have told me they were coming over." Alcott's expression was serious when he looked at Henry again. "Stay here. I'll make sure everything is okay."

Henry's first instinct was to tell him to stay, too. He didn't want Alcott to be hurt.

But Alcott was his bodyguard. It was his job, and Henry knew better than to try to stop him. Instead, he watched as Alcott quickly dried his hands on a towel and put one of them on the gun he always wore at his hip, then stepped out of the kitchen.

Henry held his breath. He had no idea who was at the door or who else would have a key. Edward was the only person who came to mind, but as Alcott had said, it couldn't be him.

Henry was scared. He was frightened for himself, but also for Alcott, which meant that he cared, maybe too much. The fact that he had just broken up with Jessica didn't matter. The only thing that mattered was Alcott's safety, and Henry held his breath until Alcott finally stepped into the kitchen again.

He wasn't alone. Jessica was right behind him, and Henry frowned at the sight of her.

He'd just been thinking about her, but he didn't know what she was doing here. "Jessica?"

What was he supposed to feel looking at her for the first time since they'd broken up? Longing, maybe? Pain? All of that was there, as was the love he still felt for her. He didn't regret their breakup, though. He'd been hurt when she'd broken their engagement, but he'd come to see it was the best thing, possibly for both of them. If she couldn't handle them not being mates, they shouldn't be together.

She stepped toward Henry, a tremulous smile on her face. "Henry. I wanted to talk to you."

Henry looked at Alcott. He didn't know what to do. He didn't want to talk to her, but it would be rude to kick her out without listening to what she had to say. He felt he owed it to her, even though he didn't. "Of course," he finally answered.

Everything had been going so well, and Alcott realized he should have known this would happen. He and Henry had been in the kitchen, working together as if they belonged together. It had felt coupley, and even though Alcott had known that wasn't the case, he'd allowed himself to believe it for a moment. Henry was safe, and they were together — had been together for a while. They were comfortable, and it showed as they moved around the kitchen, handing things to each other, understanding each other without talking.

Then he'd heard the sound of someone trying to open the front door, and here they were. Henry looked lost when he saw Jessica, and it was easy for Alcott to imagine what he was feeling. He was confused but also happy to see his ex-fiancée.

As for Jessica, Alcott had no idea why she was here. She hadn't told him, instead saying that she wanted to talk to Henry. Alcott was tempted to say no, to use his job as Henry's bodyguard to keep her way. Henry wouldn't thank him for that, though, and it would only delay the inevitable.

Alcott cleared his throat. "I'm going to leave the two of you alone." He was jealous, and it was a problem.

A *big* problem

Henry's eyes widened. "Are you sure?"

"Jessica said she wanted to talk to you, and I don't see a problem with that."

"You won't be far, though, will you?"

It was tempting to tell him he would be within hearing distance, but Alcott didn't want to be. He didn't want to hear whatever Jessica had to say to Henry, or the sound of them making up and getting back together, which he was pretty sure was about to happen.

He couldn't leave Henry alone, though, not even with Jessica. It was dangerous, and Alcott didn't care if he offended Jessica. She probably had nothing to do with Purity, but Alcott wasn't going to risk it. "I'll be in the living room."

"All right. Thank you. I'm sorry about this. We can eat later."

Alcott forced himself to smile. "Don't worry about me. Take your time."

Alcott wasn't hungry anymore.

He ignored the way Jessica was staring at him and headed to the living room. He didn't want to leave them alone, but they had to talk. Alcott had been there when their relationship had imploded, and he knew they hadn't talked since then. Jessica had been angry, sad, and she hadn't wanted to see Henry. It looked like she'd changed her mind, and it sucked, big time.

Alcott should be happy. He should want *Henry* to be happy.

He was almost at the kitchen door when a hand touched his shoulder. He turned around to see Henry standing there, his head cocked, a frown on his face. "Are you okay?" Henry asked.

Alcott cleared his throat. "A bit worried, but I don't think she has anything to do with Purity."

Henry's frown deepened instead of smoothing out. "Is that the only reason you're worried?"

Alcott sucked in a breath. Did Henry know something? Had he realized how Alcott felt about him? Alcott wanted to think no, to believe he was better than that at hiding his feelings, but he wasn't sure. Henry was Henry. Alcott felt so comfortable with him that maybe he hadn't been careful. Henry wasn't just a job, and Alcott hadn't been acting like he was. Henry might know how he felt and that he was worried about him because of that.

He forced a smile onto his face. "I'm fine. Focus on yourself and your relationship."

Henry shook his head. "I don't have a relationship with her anymore," he murmured low enough that Jessica wouldn't hear him.

"Maybe you do. Why do you think she's here?"

Henry looked nonplussed. "You think she wants to get back with me?"

"It would make sense. I know the way you left each other wasn't great and that she made a lot of mistakes. It doesn't mean you can't be together, though."

"But we can't. We're not mates."

"So? I don't see why that should stop you from being together." Alcott's heart felt like it was breaking, but he had to say the words. He had to reassure Henry when it was obvious Henry needed to be reassured.

"That's true," Henry said slowly. "You don't have to be mates with someone to love them and be with them."

"Exactly." Alcott's heart was breaking in his chest. He should have seen this coming. Maybe it was time to call Dakota and ask him to replace him. He'd wanted to take care of Henry on his own, and so far, it had worked out. He wasn't sure he could still do it, that he could watch Henry and Jessica be happy together.

He was happy for Henry, but his heart broke every time he thought of the two of them together. He wasn't going to say anything to Henry, although he would have to find a reason why he wasn't his bodyguard anymore and why he was staying away.

All of that could come later, though. Right now, Henry had to talk to Jessica.

"Are you sure you're okay?" Henry asked.

Alcott hoped the smile on his face didn't look like a grimace. "I'm fine. And don't worry. She's not with Purity."

"That's not what I was worried about. I was worried about

you. You look different. Sad."

Dammit. Alcott needed to keep his expression under control. He'd been trained to do it. Why couldn't he do it when he was with Henry? "I'm fine. A bit worried, but I'm sure you understand that. Focus on her. That's what you need to do right now."

"Focusing on her doesn't mean I can't focus on you. You're my friend, Alcott. I'm worried."

"You don't have to be. I promise."

That didn't seem to reassure Henry as much as Alcott hoped, but there was nothing else Alcott could tell him. He quickly squeezed the hand Henry still had on his shoulder, then he stepped away. "I'll be in the living room," he said, loud enough that Jessica could hear him. "If you need anything, just call, and I'll be there in seconds." He forced himself to look at Jessica. "That goes for you, too. I won't be listening in, but I won't be far."

Jessica frowned. "I'm not sure why you're telling me that, but fine." She was cold, something she wasn't usually, but Alcott could understand. She wanted to talk to Henry, and Alcott wasn't leaving. He was disturbing her plans, and while he wanted to continue doing it, possibly to show her the door and ask her to leave, he couldn't.

He turned toward the kitchen door, but before leaving, he looked at Henry one last time.

Henry wasn't looking at him anymore. He was staring at Jessica and frowning as if he was trying to read her. Maybe he was. He didn't like being surprised.

Alcott didn't like it either in this case.

Henry didn't know what to say, which wasn't something that happened often. Jessica had stunned him by coming today, and he had no idea what she wanted. Part of him wondered if she'd decided she wanted him back, but that couldn't be it. He didn't know what he would answer if that were the case.

Or rather, he knew what he would answer, and just the thought of doing it made him nervous.

"I didn't expect to see you here today," he said because they were just staring at each other, and one of them had to take the first step.

Jessica smiled awkwardly. "I wasn't sure I would be welcome."

"You will always be welcome. Even though we're not together anymore, we're friends." That wasn't exactly true. They'd been friends before they'd become a couple, but he doubted they would continue being friends now. It was awkward, especially after the way things had ended between them.

She smiled softly, and it reminded Henry of other situations and happier memories.

They were just that, though. Memories, moments he would never get back. Something had broken between them, and they couldn't get it back. He loved her still, with that soft kind of love that was reserved to siblings, to friends who weren't friends anymore.

Now, he was terrified about why she was here.

"I wanted to talk to you." She sucked in a breath. "I'm sorry." She pulled on a strand of her hair, a gesture he'd seen so often that it made his heart ache.

He'd lost a lot when Jessica had walked out of their relationship, and he still hurt over it. He'd thought they would spend the rest of their lives together, that they would be friends, companions, lovers. She'd broken all of that with one word, with her need to find out if they were mates. Henry had been afraid, but he'd given in, just like he'd given in too often when it came to her. He knew he shouldn't have, but it was too late.

He cleared his throat. "I'm listening."

"You're not going to make this easy on me, are you?"

"I don't know what you're talking about. Why are you here, Jessie?"

She blinked at the familiar nickname, but she didn't say anything about it. Instead, she started, "I had time to think about what happened."

She sounded unsure, and while Henry's first instinct was to help her say the things she was thinking, he stayed quiet. This was her game. She was the one making the rules, and he followed.

She flashed him a smile. "I'm sorry for the way I behaved. I shouldn't have pushed to find out if we were mates, and I shouldn't have left when we found out we weren't. Being mates doesn't matter. I should have known that, and instead, I allowed old stories to influence me. We love each other, and that's the only important thing."

Henry had no idea what to tell her. "What are you saying?" he asked, hoping it would give him more time. He didn't want to hurt Jessica, but he was going to have to.

"I talked to your grandfather," Jessica said.

That was the last thing Henry had expected to hear from her. It instantly wiped the smile from his face, and he straightened. "What do you mean, you talked to my grandfather?"

Jessica's eyes widened, but thankfully, she explained, "Just that. He contacted me when he found out we weren't going to get married anymore. He asked me what happened. I told him, and he made me see that I shouldn't put that much faith in the mate bond. He said it was ridiculous and that I was the perfect woman for you, that we love each other, and that we had to keep that in mind rather than antiquated traditions."

Henry snorted. "Antiquated traditions? You think that finding your mate is an antiquated tradition?"

Her cheeks pinked. "Not exactly, no. I do realize I was

romanticizing that kind of relationship, though. I should have focused on how I felt about you, on how much I love you, not on how much I want us to be mates. Your grandfather isn't wrong, Henry. Being mates doesn't mean anything. Most element wielders never find their mates, and they're fine with the lives they live. I don't see why I should be different."

"Did he push you into this?" Henry had to ask. He wouldn't put it past Melchior.

"Of course not. I never stopped loving you, even though I broke up with you. I told you I shouldn't have done it. I acted on the pain I was feeling. I regretted it almost instantly, but I stayed away because I didn't think you'd want to listen to me. I thought I'd hurt you too much."

"And you don't think that anymore?"

She looked away. "I *know* I hurt you, and I regret it. It's one of the biggest regrets I'll ever have. I hope we can get over it, though. I love you, Henry, and I know you love me. You told me enough times when you tried to talk me through this and before. I will never be sorry enough for what I did, but I want us to put it behind us. I want us to get married like we were planning to."

Henry shook his head. "We can't. I canceled everything."

"But we can get married later, or maybe with a smaller ceremony. It doesn't matter as long as I'm with you."

She sounded so earnest that Henry had to wonder if she really wanted this. He couldn't stop thinking about the fact that his grandfather had talked to her. He should have known Melchior would stick his nose into it. This was what he wanted, wasn't it? He couldn't be in charge of the company. He hadn't been in years, and he detested Henry and Edward for taking their father's place as CEO. He wanted his power back, as well as the company, but he couldn't, so he was sticking his nose into his grandkids' lives.

Henry would have none of that. He barely talked to

Melchior, and he didn't want that to change, but it would have to.

"What changed?" he asked. "Is it only that you realized being mates doesn't matter? Or is it because you missed me, or maybe you didn't want to be alone?"

"I missed you. It doesn't have anything to do with being alone. I love you, and I should never have left you."

Henry shook his head. He understood where she was coming from. He'd missed her, too, and he still did some days. But he'd come to realize that what he missed more was the idea of her, of being in a relationship. They'd been together for so long that their lives had melded together, and now that they weren't anymore, it was hard to fill the holes she had left. It was as if Henry's life was half empty, and he didn't know what to do with that.

He did know that getting back with Jessica wasn't a good idea, though. It didn't only have to do with the fact that his grandfather approved of the marriage. He didn't care whether or not Melchior approved. But if Melchior was pushing for it, it meant he had a good reason to, and it was one more reason for Henry to stay away from Jessica. It wasn't the only one, though. When she'd broken up with him, she'd broken something between them, and he doubted they could ever get it back.

"I'm sorry," he murmured.

She took a step closer, reaching for him but not touching him. "What are you sorry for? We can be happy together. We were. Nothing has to change. I know you need time to forgive me, and I can give that to you."

"It's not only that." Henry didn't know how to tell her. He didn't know if he *could* tell her.

He'd missed her and their relationship, but he'd moved on, or at least, he'd started to. He had Alcott, even though he didn't know whether or not they could have more than friendship. He knew he wanted to, though, and that it wasn't only physical.

He wanted Alcott the way they'd been together in the kitchen earlier. He wanted them to share a home, a life. He loved the way they fit together, and he loved Alcott. It might be too soon, but he was sure it wasn't a rebound. No matter how much he loved Jessica, his love had changed. It wasn't a husband kind of love anymore, which was what he felt for Alcott. It might make him an asshole, but he couldn't change the way he felt, and he wouldn't give in just because he felt guilty.

He swallowed. "I'm sorry," he repeated. "I love you and miss you, and I think part of me will always wonder what we could have had. I don't want to get back with you, though."

"Why?" Jessica sounded hurt. She wrapped her arms around herself and stared at Henry, waiting for an answer.

Henry didn't want to hurt her, even though she had hurt him. "Because I've changed."

"We only broke up weeks ago. How much can you have changed?"

"It's not only that. I don't think our relationship meant as much to you is it did to me." Or maybe it hadn't meant much to either of them to begin with. He hadn't realized that until she left him, but even though he missed her, he also felt free to try to be himself again. It sounded callous, but he couldn't deny it.

Jessica was the perfect woman for him, at least from his grandfather's point of view, and Henry had thought that, too. She would be good on his arm as company parties. She would be the perfect CEO's wife — beautiful, intelligent, smart, good at conversations, and at putting people at ease.

She wouldn't be the perfect wife for Henry, though.

Alcott was pacing on the balcony. He couldn't think about what was going on inside the apartment. He'd told Henry he would be in the living room, but he'd still been able to hear what was happening in the kitchen from there, so he'd left.

He shouldn't have, but he didn't think Jessica was here to hurt Henry. Hell, she'd told Henry she wanted to get back with him. Alcott had expected it, but it didn't hurt less. He should have talked to Henry before. He shouldn't have waited until this happened. Now, Henry and Jessica were getting back together, and they would probably get married soon, while Alcott watched from afar.

He'd been an idiot. He'd been a *coward*, afraid of losing Henry's friendship, and now he wasn't sure he could keep it anyway. He had no doubt Henry would try to be friends with him, but he knew he couldn't stand to the side, watching Henry and Jessica be happy, getting married and maybe having kids. It was selfish of him, and maybe with time, he would be able to get over his feelings. It wouldn't happen right away, though, which meant he would have to stay away from Henry, at least for now. He was tempted to call Dakota and ask him for a replacement bodyguard, but first, he wanted to talk to Henry. No matter how much it hurt, he wouldn't abandon Henry.

He turned around and paced the other way, looking at the open living room door. He should get back inside. He should be there, smiling, understanding, welcoming Jessica back in Henry's life—only to leave it himself. He could do it.

He would have to.

He heard the front door open and frowned. He moved toward it, needing to check who was leaving or coming in, but before he could get there, Henry stepped into the living room. They stared at each other, and Alcott tried to read Henry's expression. He wasn't smiling, which was a surprise. Shouldn't he be smiling since he'd just gotten back with his fiancée? And where was Jessica?

Alcott cleared his throat. "Do you have something to do?"

Henry shrugged. "No."

Alcott blinked. He didn't understand what was happening. "Is everything okay?"

Henry sighed and walked closer. "I don't know. I'm fine, but it's going to take her some time to be okay, and I have to talk to my grandfather."

"I heard she talked to him."

Henry cocked his head, watching Alcott. "You were listening in?"

"Not exactly. I told you I'd stay in the living room, and I intended to do just that, but I could still hear you. That's why I moved outside onto the balcony. I only came in when I heard the door. I wanted to check who it was."

Henry nodded. "It was Jessica. She left."

Alcott wanted to ask him what had happened, but he didn't. Henry would tell him if he wanted him to know. Still, he had to know if Jessica was going to come around. "Should I expect her to come back?" he asked, hoping his voice was calm and steady. He wasn't sure he managed, though, from the little smile that bloomed on Henry's lips.

"I don't think she will, no. I told her we were better separated than together."

Alcott's chest felt like it was about to burst open. "You did?"

Henry nodded and pushed by Alcott so he could step onto the balcony. He took a deep breath, and his shoulders visibly relaxed. "She wanted to get back with me. She apologized and told me she shouldn't have put that much importance on us being mates. She also told me she talked to my grandfather and that he approved of her getting back with me."

"You didn't say no only to spite him, did you?" Alcott didn't know what was going on between Henry and Edward and their grandfather, but he knew there was bad blood there.

Henry snorted. "God, no. If I wanted to get back with Jessica, I would, no matter what he thinks."

"But you didn't want to get back with her?" Alcott held his breath, wondering how Henry was going to answer.

"I didn't. I might have wanted to in the beginning, but I'm over that."

"You were together for years. How can you be over it?"

"I don't know. She hurt me a lot when she broke up with me, especially because of why she did it. I couldn't believe she would waste everything we'd built because we weren't meant to be together. I mean, it's ridiculous. We don't even know how it works or why we have mates. So yes, I was angry. But the breakup made me see that maybe it was for the best. I loved her, and I still do, but it's not the kind of love I associate with someone I want to marry."

Alcott had to lick his lips. His mouth was dry, and he wanted something to drink, but he wasn't about to leave this conversation. "Love changes. I doubt people who have been married for decades still feel the same way they did at the beginning of their relationship."

"You're right. Maybe I'm wrong, but I know I don't want to marry her anymore, and I don't want to be with her. She left me, and while I was horrified and sad in the beginning, I started developing feelings for someone else. A lot of people will say it's too soon, that it's a rebound, but it really isn't. I think we can love more than one person in the same way, and at the same time. I see how it could be a problem, but I can't be sure how this person will react."

Alcott's heart was racing, and it felt like it was about to jump out of his chest and throw itself at Henry. That would be messy, to say the least. "You're in love with someone else?"

Henry finally looked at Alcott. "I am. It was a surprise, but I don't regret it. I don't regret anything that happened, not when it comes to my personal life."

"Maybe you should take time, though." And maybe Alcott should stop trying to shoot himself in the foot. He wasn't sure whether or not Henry was talking about him, but he believed there was a good chance he was.

Henry shook his head. "A lot of things have changed in the past few weeks. My fiancée broke up with me. I was threatened and attacked. My brother was attacked, beaten, and found his mate. I lost my best friend. It feels like I've lived a lifetime in only a few weeks, and I think the same goes for those feelings. Maybe I wouldn't have fallen in love with this person as fast as I did if the circumstances had been different, but they weren't. They were what they were, and my feelings are what they are."

Alcott didn't know what to say. He wanted to move closer, but he still wasn't sure Henry was talking about him. He had to ask, though. He couldn't allow hope to swell in his chest if he wasn't the person Henry loved. Maybe he'd fallen in love with his secretary. Maybe he had a crush on Bay, or Dakota. Alcott had no way to know, or rather, he only had one — asking Henry.

He stepped closer. He didn't touch Henry, but he was close enough to do it. "Who did you fall in love with?" he asked, his voice only a whisper.

Henry smiled at him, looking so happy and gorgeous. "Haven't you realized? I'm talking about you."

Alcott released the breath he'd been holding. He breathed easier, even though he still wasn't sure what to do. "You're in love with me?"

"I've been for a while, even though I didn't recognize it. I was too busy focusing on other things, you know, like being threatened and almost killed. But yes. I fell in love with you, and I don't know how it happened or why. I don't think it matters, either." He hesitated. "Unless you don't share my feelings. I don't expect anything from you, Alcott. We can keep our relationship strictly a professional and friendly one if that's what you want. I'm in love with you, but it doesn't mean you have to love me back. I'll understand if you don't, and I won't try to hurt you."

"I already know that." Alcott stepped even closer, and when he reached for Henry's face, Henry didn't move away. He allowed Alcott to cup his cheek, to bring him even closer, and wrapped an arm around his back. "I love you too," Alcott finally admitted. "Like you, I don't know when it happened or how, but I don't care. I only care that I love you, and that you love me back."

Henry's smile was glorious. "I do." Then, he leaned even closer, and he kissed Alcott.

CHAPTER FIVE

Henry shouldn't have been as happy as he was, considering the situation, but he couldn't help the smile on his face. It was all thanks to Alcott. He'd always been there for Henry, since the first time they'd met, but there was more to it now.

Alcott loved Henry, and Henry was pretty sure he loved Alcott. He didn't know how it had happened, and he didn't think it mattered. People were going to talk. They would have things to say about Henry suddenly dumping his fiancée and popping up with a boyfriend, but Henry didn't care about that. He didn't care about anything that wasn't Alcott, Edward, and their few friends. What everyone else thought wouldn't influence how he felt.

He peeked at Alcott, who was driving. They were meeting Edward and Bay, and Henry was excited. He hadn't yet told Edward what had happened between him and Alcott. He hadn't told anyone. They'd been wrapped up in each other since Jessica had left the day before, and even though they'd done nothing more than kissing, it felt so good. It was a distraction, which made Henry slightly nervous, but he couldn't bring himself to want to stop.

Yes, he was a distraction when it came to Alcott. But Alcott knew what he was doing. Being a bodyguard was his job, and he loved Henry. Surely he would do everything he could to protect him? They had to talk about it, but Henry didn't want to. He was afraid Alcott would change his mind, that he would decide they couldn't be together because of what was going on with Purity. It made Henry want to find out about Purity even more, but they still had no clues about who might be behind it.

It felt right, though. Being with Alcott had felt right since the beginning, and now Henry knew he hadn't been wrong about it. He wanted this, much more than anything else except his safety and Edward's.

"You're thinking hard," Alcott said without looking at Henry.

Henry found himself smiling and blushing at the same time. "Sorry. It's just hard to wrap my mind around the fact that we're together."

Alcott briefly looked at him. "Regrets?"

Henry sucked in a breath. "Of course not. Why would I regret being with you?"

"I don't know. You haven't been single for long, and this was a surprise. You might have agreed to be with me in the heat of the moment, and now that you have time to think about it, you might change your mind." He hesitated. "I wouldn't hold it against you, Henry. I don't demand anything from you, or expect anything. I understand the situation is far from ideal, and if you'd rather spend some time alone, then I'll take a step back."

"Would you ask Dakota to send another bodyguard to protect me?"

Alcott bit his lower lip, and it was enough to answer Henry's question. Still, he waited. He didn't want to assume anything. "I wouldn't want to," Alcott finally said. "I *don't* want to. It would be best if I did, though. I don't know if I can be objective when it comes to your safety."

"Bay didn't ask to be taken off the case when he realized he and Edward were mates," Henry pointed out.

"Maybe he's better at this than I am. I don't know. I didn't react the right way yesterday when Jessica came. I should have stayed in the living room and listened. Instead, I was on the balcony, and I might have been too late getting to you if something had happened."

Henry frowned. "You already knew Jessica wouldn't hurt me."

"I didn't think she would, no, but how could I be sure? We know there's a mole in your office. There could be one in your personal life, too."

Henry shook his head. He might not know what was going through Jessica's mind, why she'd talked to his grandfather, but she wasn't part of Purity. That much, he was sure of. "So you made a mistake. Why?"

Alcott looked like he didn't want to answer, but he sucked in a breath and admitted, "I thought you were going to get back with her, and I didn't want to listen to that."

It made something in Henry's heart soften. He wanted to reach out, to take Alcott's hand, and he could now, couldn't he? He did just that, briefly squeezing it before letting go. Alcott was driving, and Henry didn't want to distract him. "Well, now you know I won't be getting back with her."

Alcott smiled. "Now I know. I just want you to be aware of the fact that you can take a step back if that's what you want. I won't hold it against you. I want you to feel comfortable with me."

"And you don't expect anything." Henry didn't like that. If they were together, Alcott *should* expect things from him. He did understand that the situation made everything harder, though, so he wasn't going to fight Alcott on that, at least not yet.

"Exactly. We can figure things out as we go."

That sounded good. Henry didn't know what he was doing, and he suspected Alcott didn't, either. Being together felt natural, but with everything else in their lives, it wouldn't be. Henry had to think of the company, of Edward, probably of his grandfather, too, who would pitch a fit when he found out that Henry was with a man and not with a woman that he approved of. Alcott, on the other hand, had to deal with the fact that he was Henry's bodyguard and that Dakota might want to take him off the case.

But they could do this. Henry was sure of it.

They finally got to Edward's building, and Henry sat straighter. He hadn't told his brother what had happened, but he knew he would as soon as he saw Edward. They were close, more best friends than brothers, and he would never hide anything from him. He hoped Edward would be happy for him, and he thought that would be the case. Edward might have doubts, though. He liked Jessica, and he would wonder if Henry wasn't rushing into his new relationship. And maybe he was. He didn't think it mattered, though. It felt right, and that was that.

Henry and Alcott were silent in the elevator. They stood closer than they would have yesterday, and it made Henry smile. Their arms brushed together every time one of them moved, and they couldn't seem to help but look at each other and smile every time it happened. Henry felt guilty for distracting Alcott, and he knew it was dangerous. He had to be careful with Purity on the prowl, but he wanted this for himself, at least for a bit. He wanted to be happy and to take his time.

The elevator doors opened, and Bay was already there, waiting for them with the apartment door ajar. He saw the way they were standing close to each other and arched a brow, but he didn't say anything about it, and he didn't try to stop Henry when he rushed into the apartment, looking for his brother. He found Edward where he'd been the last time — on the couch, looking grumpy. His expression softened when he saw Henry. Then, his eyes widened. "What happened?" he asked.

Henry laughed. "Why do you think something happened?"

"I can see it in your expression. What is it?"

Henry looked at the living room door, but neither Bay nor Alcott were there. He suspected they wanted to give him and Edward some time alone, and that was more than fine with him. "Something happened yesterday," he admitted as he sat by Edward's feet.

"Are you not going to tell me what?"

"Jessica came to the apartment yesterday. She wanted to get back with me."

Edward's expression shifted. "Why? She didn't want to be with you because you're not mates. What changed?"

Henry scowled. "Apparently, she talked to Melchior."

"Why would she want to do that?"

"I don't know, but I intend to find out."

Edward's eyes widened. "You're not going to talk to him, are you?"

"I am. What I do with my personal life, or even with the company, isn't his business. I won't let that go."

"It won't help. You know that."

"I don't care. I want him to know that he has to leave me alone." Henry smiled again. "Because he's going to be pissed when he finds out that Alcott and I are together."

Edward squeaked and tried to kick Henry. "You couldn't have started with that?"

"I'm sorry. I thought you should know about Melchior."

Edward shook his head, but he was smiling. "And I'm glad you told me. I should also know that my brother has a boyfriend, though. What happened? Did you finally realize he was in love with you?"

"Realize? He told me. Well, after I told him I wouldn't be getting back with Jessica and that I was in love with someone else."

Edward shook his head fondly. "It was obvious, but of course you didn't see it. He's been in love with you for a while." He reached out, taking one of Henry's hands. "I'm happy for you."

"You don't think it's too soon?"

Edward shrugged. "If you don't think it is, then I don't, either. As long as you and Alcott are happy, I don't see a problem with it." He paused and grimaced. "Melchior will, though. And you know he *will* find out."

"That's why I need to confront him. I want him to know that I won't tolerate any kind of invasion of my privacy, any kind of attempt from him to influence the company or me." It wasn't the first time Melchior had tried it. Henry had never seen him as angry as he had been when the company had kicked him out as CEO, but he knew that might change when he saw him. He didn't care. He was ready for a fight if that was what Melchior wanted.

"We want to visit our grandfather," Henry said as he and Edward walked into the kitchen.

Alcott blinked. He was curious to find out where the bad blood between Edward and Henry and their grandfather came from, but he didn't know why they wanted to visit the man. He looked at Bay, who seemed as puzzled as he was.

"I didn't know you had a grandfather," Bay told Edward.

Edward grimaced. "I wish we didn't, but we do."

That was more than enough for Alcott and Bay to realize something was wrong with the grandfather, whoever he was. They looked at each other again. If they could avoid it, Alcott thought it would be better. He knew he wouldn't change the brothers' minds, though, not if they were intent on this. "Why don't you tell us about him?" he asked.

Bay pushed away from the table where he and Alcott were

sitting, and Edward slipped into his lap. Bay wrapped his arms around him and held him close, and while Alcott wished he could do the same with Henry, he didn't. It was too soon for them. He did take Henry's hand when he sat next to him, though, and Henry smiled gratefully. It made Alcott feel better. They were still finding their way around each other, but they knew they both wanted to be together, and that was the most important thing.

"He was kicked out of the company several years ago," Edward said.

Alcott frowned. "Who created the company?"

"He did," Henry took over. "He was the CEO for decades, and he trained my father to take his place. It shouldn't have happened so soon, but he was making decisions people didn't agree with."

"What do you mean?"

Henry grimaced. "Let's just say that he's not the best person. He's homophobic, racist, and misogynistic. He wants everyone in the company to be male, white, and an earth wielder. He didn't want us to hire humans, even though there aren't enough earth wielders in the city, or maybe not even in the state, for us to work with. He fired people he didn't like without reason. He was handsy with the ladies who worked at the office, things like that. Edward and I were young then, so we don't know the details, but our father talked with people he trusted, and they decided my grandfather had to step down. He wasn't happy about it."

Edward snorted. "That's an understatement. He was *pissed*. The company was his, and no one else's. Even though he'd been training our father to take his place, it wasn't supposed to happen until he died. Then he found himself kicked out. He put up a fight, but he lost. He tried to do the same when our father died and we inherited the company, but no one wanted him back. We won again, and he's been trying to

stick his nose into our lives ever since. It's not anything out-
rageous because he doesn't like to talk to us, but he does
things like talking to Jessica and trying to convince her to get
back with Henry."

Alcott had told Bay what had happened, so he didn't ask
what was going on when it came to the relationship between
Henry and Jessica. He knew Jessica had come by and that
Henry wasn't going to get back with her. He was frowning,
though. "Why would you want to talk to him if you don't like
him, and he doesn't like you?" he asked, looking at Edward.

Edward looked at Henry, and they waited for Henry to answer.

Henry sighed. "It's not that I want to talk to him. Trust me,
if I could avoid it, I would. But he has to know he can't stick
his nose into my private life. Because if he continues doing it,
he's going to try to intervene in the business, too, and that's
not something we can allow to happen. I need to tell him to
stay out of my life, and I need to do it soon. He's probably
waiting for Jessica to call him, maybe expects us to be back
together. Either way, he's going to expect a reaction from me,
and I have to give it to him. Otherwise, he'll think that he can
do whatever he wants and I won't react, and that's the last
thing I want."

Henry and Edward couldn't afford any more problems,
not with Purity still around. If they could placate their grandfather and keep him away, it would be a good thing. Still, Alcott didn't like the sound of it. He probably shouldn't worry
about an old man, but there was no way to know whether or
not he had anything to do with Purity, or how he would react
to Edward and Henry's presence.

He looked at Bay, and he knew Bay was thinking the same.

He cleared his throat. "You're willing to fight your family
for this? For us?" It wasn't unexpected, but it made Alcott's
throat tight with emotion.

Henry shrugged. "Melchior isn't my family. Edward is. You are. I'm not going to fight him. I'm just going to tell him to fuck off and leave me alone."

Edward chuckled and reached out to pat Henry's shoulder. "You know things are getting serious when Henry starts cussing. We promise we'll be careful, but Henry's right. It has to be done. We don't have a relationship with Melchior, and he has no business talking to Jessica, and he probably had a secret reason to do it. We should find out what it is before he gets what he wants and springs it on us."

"I don't think that's the case," Henry intervened. "I think he wanted Jessica to get back with me because she's an earth wielder, and she would be the perfect CEO's wife. He doesn't care what either of us feels or if we love each other. He doesn't think love has anything to do with marriage. He just wants us to get back together because it will look good, and because he thinks I need to father a child so the boy can take my place in the company when I die."

Alcott hesitated. He knew that Henry wouldn't change his mind about being with him, but he made it sound like their relationship would complicate things. "What will he have to say about you having a boyfriend? And worse, having a boyfriend who doesn't wield the same element as you do?"

Henry shrugged. "I don't give a fuck."

That answered Alcott's questions. He still wasn't crazy about it, but if the brothers had to do it, they should. He and Bay weren't just their bodyguards anymore. They were with Henry and Edward, part of their little family, as Henry had just said. They had to protect them, yes, but also to support them and the decisions they made about their lives. If they wanted to talk to this man, then they should. "When do you want to go?" Alcott asked.

Edward and Henry looked at each other again. "The sooner we do this, the better," Henry said. "He's probably waiting for me or Jessica to call him to tell him what happened, and if we don't, he'll know something is wrong. He might try something else, which is the last thing we need."

"You want to go now?" Edward asked.

"If you're up to it, yes. I don't think we have a reason to wait."

The four of them looked at each other. "Let's go, then," Alcott said with a sigh.

He didn't like it, but it apparently was necessary, and he wouldn't hold Henry back. He'd promised himself he wouldn't when they'd decided to be together, and he wasn't going to break that promise, not if he could help it. Henry knew what he was doing when it came to his company, while Alcott was utterly lost. He had to let Henry take the lead on it, no matter how anxious it made him feel.

Henry barely looked at the house when the four of them arrived. He hadn't grown up there. His parents had wanted a smaller place, a place where they could be a family instead of this estate, and Henry was glad. He wouldn't have felt comfortable here, especially with his grandfather around — and he would have been around.

He always tried to stick his nose into the family affairs. He thought it was his right, since he considered himself the patriarch. Henry and Edward's father hadn't agreed, which was why he'd moved his family. He wanted them to have their own space without Melchior hovering over them, trying to order them around. It had been the best choice, and it had meant that Edward and Henry had grown up without Melchior. They knew who he was, of course, and they saw him several times a year, but he wasn't truly a grandfather. Henry still wondered how his father had managed to come out of that. He'd been a good man, nothing like Melchior. It probably had been his grandmother's influence, although Henry wouldn't know, since she'd died before he was even born.

It didn't matter anyway. Henry's father had been a good man, and his grandfather wasn't. Henry had to make sure Melchior stayed away, and that was that.

He and Edward looked at each other as they stood in the entrance. Edward was still a bit shaky and still bruised, but he wanted to be here, and Henry hadn't said no. He probably should have, but he knew he would need the support. He was used to facing off with Melchior, but now he felt vulnerable. He had Alcott, and he had to protect him against Melchior. Alcott might not realize it was necessary, but Henry did, and he knew Melchior wouldn't be happy at finding out that both he and Edward were with a man, moreover, with men who didn't wield the same element as they did. As far as Melchior was concerned, they were fucking up their lives, and he was going to try to straighten them out.

It wouldn't work.

A door slammed in the distance, and Henry looked toward the sound. "Where do you think he is?" They could probably look for Melchior in the house for days and not find him. It was that big.

Edward shrugged. "His office?"

"We should start there."

Before they could move, though, a redheaded man walked into the entrance. He startled and took a step back, then smiled when he recognized them. "Henry, Edward. I didn't expect you." He frowned. "Melchior didn't say anything about you coming."

Matias was the son of Melchior's secretary, Caitlin. Henry wasn't sure why Melchior needed a secretary, but he wasn't about to ask. As long as he stayed out of Henry's life, he could do whatever he wanted.

"We'd like to talk to our grandfather," Edward explained.

He'd always had a soft spot for Matias, who didn't look like he belonged here. The only reason he was here was that his mother worked for Melchior, and he'd been coming around since he was a child. He wasn't anymore, though, and he stood tall, with his red hair, brown eyes, and freckles. He was kind of adorable, and Henry might not be close to him, but he still viewed him a bit like a little brother. Matias didn't have anyone but his mother, and from what Henry had seen, she wasn't the greatest mother in the world.

"He's in his office," Matias confirmed. "I'm sure you remember where it is."

"We do. You should stay down here."

Matias frowned, his gaze moving to Bay and Alcott, who were standing behind Edward and Henry. "Is anything wrong?"

Henry didn't want to scare him. "Not wrong exactly, but Melchior is probably going to start yelling soon, and I'm sure you'll want to stay out of his way."

Matias grimaced. "Thanks for the warning. I'll make sure to be on the other side of the house, then."

"You do that."

Matias hesitated. "What has he done now?" he asked.

"He called my ex-fiancée and tried to convince her to get back with me," Henry explained. There was probably more to the situation, but he didn't want to give Matias details. He didn't need them.

"That sounds like him, all right. I'm sorry he did that, Henry."

"Don't worry about it. You had nothing to do with it, which is why I suggest you stay away from his office for a bit."

"That won't be a problem. Thanks again for the warning." He waved at them and left.

Henry turned to Edward. "Ready?"

"As ready as I ever will be, I guess. We might as well do it now."

So they did. They climbed the stairs in the entrance hall, getting to the first floor of the house. It was where Melchior's huge office was located, and sure enough, he was there when they knocked on the door. He was behind his desk, talking to his secretary, but he stopped as soon as he saw them. He didn't get up—it was a subtle insult, telling them that he didn't respect them enough to get up when they came in, but Henry didn't care. He wasn't about to shake his grandfather's hand anyway. Melchior didn't respect them, and they didn't respect him.

"Boys. To what do I owe this pleasure?" Melchior asked. His gaze stopped on Henry, and he grinned. "Have good news for me?"

"It depends on what you think is good news. I'm not getting back with Jessica, Melchior. It doesn't matter that you called her."

Melchior's smile faded. "Why not? I had to work hard to convince her. Why did you ruin everything again?"

"Because there's a reason Jessica and I broke up."

"She told me. You aren't mates, and she was sad about it. Bullshit. Who cares if you're mates or not? It doesn't mean you can't get married."

"Because marriage doesn't have anything to do with love."

"Exactly. It has to do with business, with the way you look. She'll be the perfect wife for you."

That was what Henry had thought. "She might be, but I'm not going to marry her. I don't love her anymore."

"Who cares about love? I didn't love your grandmother."

"But our father loved our mother, and I want to love the person I will be marrying." It was way too soon to talk about marriage with Alcott, of course, but maybe, eventually. It was easier to see himself married to him than to Jessica, that was for sure.

Henry was starting to suspect that he'd asked her to marry him because it was what everyone had expected him to do rather than because he wanted to. He loved her, so it hadn't been that much of a problem, but now, he realized there should be more to marriage. He hadn't been *in* love with her. He'd wanted to do what was right, and as he did so, he'd forgotten about himself. He was glad Jessica had broken up with him. He would have realized this too late—after they were married, and it would have been hell, both for him and her.

"Stay away from me and Edward, and from Jessica," Henry said.

"How can I stay away when you boys don't know what you're doing? I had to do it. You need an heir, someone who will take over the company after you die."

"And I will have one." Maybe. He and Alcott hadn't talked about children, and if it was too soon to talk about marriage, talking about children would be even worse. "But if I have an heir, *I* will choose the person I will have him or her with. You have to stay out of my private life and out of the business."

"You're not a good CEO. I built that company with my blood and sweat, and you're going to ruin everything," Melchior said, finally getting to his feet.

His secretary reached for him when he stumbled, and Henry wondered when he'd started having problems being on his feet. He hadn't seen Melchior in a long time, maybe since his parents' funeral, and he hadn't even realized Melchior had health problems.

He didn't care.

"Leave us alone," Edward said. His voice was softer but just as strong as Henry's. "You're not the CEO anymore, and you never will be again. What we do with the company isn't your business. Stay away from me, and from Henry. We're trying to be happy, and that won't happen if you're in our lives."

"Happy?" Melchior asked, his voice rising. "I don't care if you're happy. I only care about the company. I won't let you ruin everything I worked so hard for."

That much had always been obvious, and Henry hadn't expected it to change. He would have to find a way to keep Melchior away, though, if not for himself, for Edward.

Bay and Alcott looked at each other. The voices in the office had started to rise, and Alcott wasn't sure what to do. He didn't want to intervene, not when it wasn't his business, but he didn't like anyone yelling at Henry, or even at Edward. He wanted to charge in there and put himself between them and their grandfather, but it was probably the worst thing he could do.

A movement at the end of the hallway made him turn around, and he frowned when he saw the kid they'd met earlier in the entrance looking at them. He gestured at Matias to come closer, and Matias looked around as if wondering if Alcott meant him or someone else in the hallway. Since the hallway was empty apart from them, it was pretty obvious who Alcott was referring to.

Alcott resisted the urge to roll his eyes and waited for Matias to come closer. "Didn't Henry tell you to leave?" he asked.

Matias grimaced. "I probably should, but I wanted to make sure they were okay. It never ends well when they fight with their grandfather. Usually, they do it on the phone, and they can hang up. It's going to be harder this time, since they're facing him."

"What is it to you?"

Bay moved closer to him, probably to caution him. Alcott realized he was on edge. It wasn't just because of the situation they were in now, though. They had no way to know if Purity was waiting for them, watching them, and he didn't like being in the open. They'd had to drive almost an hour to get to the house, which meant they'd have to drive another hour to get home. It gave Purity too many opportunities to attack.

Matias shuffled his feet. "I apologize if I did anything wrong," he said. His voice was soft, as if he was used to apologizing.

It made Alcott feel guilty. Alcott rubbed the back of his neck. "I'm sorry for being so curt. I'm just wondering who you are. Henry didn't explain."

That made Matias smile. "He's known me for what feels like my entire life, but we're not friends." He stuck his hand out, and Alcott shook it. "My name is Matias. I'm the son of Melchior's secretary."

Alcott frowned. "What are you doing here, though?"

"Well, Melchior works from home, obviously, so my mother spends all her days here. I often come with her when I'm not working, mostly so she doesn't have to drive. She's been talking about moving in with Melchior so she can be there if he needs her outside office hours, but there's nothing I want less. I'm not sure I can afford a place on my own, though."

He was telling Alcott a lot of things he probably shouldn't be telling a stranger, but it was endearing. "You don't want to move into this house?"

Matias shook his head. "It's not a house. It's more like a hotel, and to be honest, I don't like Melchior very much. I hate how he treats his grandsons. He needs my mother, but not me, so he acts as if I don't exist, which isn't the best, but way better than if he were to pay attention to me."

"Yet you keep coming."

Matias chuckled. "I don't know why. I guess it's better to be here than staying home alone. If anything, I can spend time in the library and read as much as I want. They have incredible books here."

That made sense. Alcott wasn't one for reading a lot, but he understood why Matias might be, especially if he had to stick around here for a while.

"What do you know about the relationship between the brothers and their grandfather?" Bay asked. He was staring at the door behind which Henry and Edward had disappeared as if he was ready to knock it down to get to them. He probably was, too, and Alcott wouldn't be far behind.

"I know it's not good. Melchior's relationship with his son wasn't good, either. I don't know the entire story, but he was kind of fired from the company he created. He didn't take that well, and he's been trying to find a way back into it since then."

"Do they see each other often?"

"God, no. I can't even remember the last time I saw Edward and Henry." Matias smiled deprecatingly. "Which is a pity, because I don't have many friends, and I like them, but it's none of their business, I guess."

Alcott liked this less and less, though. He could hear what was happening inside—a man's voice, it had to be Melchior's, was loud enough that it was as if Alcott was standing next to him—and he wanted to intervene. Melchior was yelling at Henry that he needed to do the right thing for the business, to marry Jessica and have a son with her. Henry was yelling back, and Alcott didn't have to hear him to know what he was saying. He wasn't about to marry anyone he didn't love, and he didn't love Jessica anymore. Things might have been different if they hadn't broken up, but they had, and now, Henry was free to marry whoever he wanted.

Maybe even Alcott one day.

Alcott couldn't think about that now, though. He had to focus on Henry's safety, which was why he was here.

He still didn't know what was going on between him and Henry, but he knew it was important and that it would change both their lives. He didn't want to lose it, especially not because of a bigoted man. It made everything more complicated, though. Alcott didn't want Henry to stay away from his grandfather because it would be safer. He wanted him to stay away from Melchior because he was afraid Melchior would change Henry's mind. He realized it was stupid, especially after the way Henry had talked about the man, but he was terrified, and he knew it had nothing to do with the situation and everything to do with his feelings.

He was in trouble. He hadn't even told Dakota that he and Henry were together, but he would have to. That way, Dakota could plan and decide what he wanted to do. He hadn't taken Bay away from Edward even when he'd found out they were mates, but that was different. They were mates, not only boyfriends. It probably wouldn't change anything from Dakota's point of view, but maybe it would. Alcott didn't know. Dakota didn't care about mates or about the kind of relationship the men he worked with had, but Henry and Edward were his friends, and he wanted Purity to be destroyed. He wouldn't allow anything to ruin that opportunity, not even Alcott's feelings.

Alcott sighed and rubbed his forehead. It was so freaking complicated.

"Everything okay?" Matias asked gently.

"Everything will be okay as soon as we leave."

Matias smiled. "I wish I could leave, too."

"Why don't you?"

Matias shrugged. "Where would I go? I only have my mother. I don't even earn enough to get my own apartment. I know it's ridiculous. I'm a man. I shouldn't be living with my mother."

"There's nothing you can do about that." Alcott didn't see

anything wrong with it, although it was clear that Matias felt trapped.

"I wish that were true. I'm sure there would be something I could do about it if I put my head to it, but I'm terrified of being alone."

Alcott understood that. He was terrified of being alone, too, and he could too easily imagine what would happen if Henry broke up with him.

He couldn't focus on that right now. He had to think about Henry's safety. That was the most important thing. Because if something happened to Henry, there would be nothing between him and Alcott. They would be nothing — period.

CHAPTER SIX

Henry had already known that whatever he said to Melchior, it wouldn't change anything. His grandfather wouldn't change his mind, not when he was convinced that he was right. Henry might not be able to make that happen, but he could make Melchior see that he was never getting back with Jessica, no matter what happened, no matter what Melchior said.

He straightened his back. "Look," he began, choosing his words carefully. "I don't care what you think of Jessica and me. We're never getting back together. I already have someone else in my life, and that's that."

Even though Henry knew Melchior was going to be pissed, he was relieved when the words gave Melchior pause. "You're dating someone else?"

"I am."

"Who? I hope it's someone better than Jessica. Maybe the daughter of another businessman?"

Henry almost snorted. Trust Melchior not to care that it had hardly been any time since Henry canceled his wedding and that he'd just been pushing for them to get back together. It made sense, though. Since love wasn't supposed to be involved in marriage, it didn't matter. Henry could have broken up with Jessica yesterday, and he would have had the same reaction from Melchior.

"He's not part of our world."

Melchior's eyes widened, and he tried to move toward Henry. His secretary had to hold him up, and she scowled at

Henry.

He didn't care. He didn't care what Melchior thought, what the woman standing with him thought. She had never approved of him and Edward anyway, and that wasn't going to change anytime soon. She might only be Melchior's secretary, but they thought alike. There was a reason she was still in his employ.

"A man?" Melchior asked, disgust dripping from the words.

"A man, and he's an air wielder."

Henry waited, wondering if his grandfather's head was about to explode. It sure looked like it might.

Melchior made a disgusted sound. "Of course you're dating a man, and not even an earth wielder. I should've known. After your father married that woman—"

"He married our mother," Edward snapped. It took a lot to make Edward angry, but Melchior always managed.

Melchior waved his words away. "I don't care who she was. She wasn't fit for the job, and you saw how that ended up."

Henry tightened his hands into fists. "Our parents loved each other, and the reason they died was that they had an accident. It had nothing to do with who our mother was."

He looked at Edward, bumping their shoulders together, and Edward knew what he was thinking even without Henry saying anything. They might as well leave. They weren't going to get anything out of Melchior, and they didn't *want* anything out of him, just for him to leave them alone.

They moved toward the door, but before they left, Edward paused and turned back to their grandfather. "By the way, I'm also dating a man, and he's a water wielder."

Then Edward opened the door and stepped out. Henry followed him, not caring one bit about whatever Melchior was yelling. Both he and Edward had known Melchior wouldn't approve of their relationships. Alcott and Bay couldn't give them children, and they didn't wield the same elements. They went against everything Melchior stood for, and Henry couldn't deny it gave him a savage satisfaction.

Bay and Alcott were standing in the hallway, along with Matias. Henry smiled at him, wondering why the poor man was still there. Henry knew he was close to his mother, although he wasn't sure why. Matias was a nice man, while his mother was anything but. Of course, Matias didn't have anyone else, so that might be the reason he was still around. Maybe it was time to change that. They had never been friends, but they were friendly, and Henry thought it was a pity that Matias had to spend time with Melchior in this mausoleum of a house.

He turned his attention to Alcott, who was staring at him as if he'd grown a second head. Henry blinked, then moved closer. "What happened?" he asked. Was it Purity? He didn't think so, because Bay and Alcott would behave differently if that were the case, but something *had* happened.

Alcott shook his head. "We heard you. You were yelling."

That didn't answer Henry's question. "So? Did you get offended about what Melchior was saying? Because you shouldn't listen to him. He's an asshole. He always has been. I'm sure you also heard what he said about our mother."

Alcott shook his head. "It's not that. You told him you had a boyfriend, that you were dating someone. You told him about me."

Henry wasn't sure why that was a problem, but he should have asked first. "I'm sorry. I didn't think you'd want to keep it a secret."

"I didn't. I don't. You can shout it from the rooftops if you want. I'm just surprised." He hesitated. "I wasn't sure whether or not we were dating. We never talked about it."

He was right. They'd kissed yesterday, had spent several

hours kissing, actually, but they hadn't talked. They obviously should have, if Alcott wasn't sure what was going on.

Henry moved even closer. He looked back at the office door, but it was closed, and he could still hear Melchior yelling on the other side of it. Melchior probably hadn't realized they were still out there, and that was a relief.

"We don't have to date if you don't want to, but I'd like us to," he told Alcott, doing his best to ignore the other three, who were no doubt staring at them.

Alcott's smile was worth doing this now, though. He shook his head, then reached for Henry. "Of course I want to date you. As long as you meant it and aren't using it only as a way to infuriate your grandfather."

Henry shook his head. He understood why Alcott might think that, but that wasn't what it was about. "I told him because I wanted him to know. He had to be aware of the fact that he can't push me around or try to find me someone else. I don't *want* anyone else. I already have you, and you're more than enough for me."

Alcott was still smiling, and Henry couldn't help but smile back.

"I'm fine with it," Alcott said. "It was just a surprise to hear you come out that way. As long as you don't regret it, I'm happy with it."

"I don't think I'll ever regret it. I have no intention of hiding you, Alcott. I don't care how long we've been together or what people think. You're mine." At least for now. Henry hoped that wouldn't change, but he had no way to know what the future would hold for them. Still, he had feelings for Alcott, was in love with him, and he was sure of the fact that he wasn't going back to Jessica, no matter what happened. That had to mean something. It had to be worth something, and he hoped the same went for Alcott.

"Why don't we head out?" Edward suggested. "I don't

know about you, but I'm not looking forward to having to face Melchior when he decides to leave the office."

Henry grimaced. "That's probably a good idea." He turned his attention to Matias. "I know it's been a while since we talked, but remember that both Edward and I are there if you need us. You have our numbers, don't you?"

Matias cocked his head as if he didn't quite understand what Henry was asking. "Yes?" he said, making it sound like a question.

"So you have our numbers?" Henry teased.

Matias's cheeks flushed. "Of course. Yes, I do have your phone numbers. I don't want to disturb you, though."

"You won't. Call us if you need anything, even if it's only a way to get away from them. I know your mother works for Melchior, but it doesn't mean you have to be here, too." Henry hesitated. He didn't want to offend Matias, but he wanted him to know about this. "And if you ever want to move away, to find your own place, or even another job, call me. I can help with that, and it won't be charity. I like you, and I hate that you have to live like this."

Matias's cheeks were so red he looked like Henry might be able to cook an egg on them. He looked away, but he was smiling. "Thank you. I'll think about it."

"Please do. I hate thinking about you in here having to listen to Melchior."

Matias chuckled. "I don't listen to him anymore. I've heard everything he has to say. But thank you. I'll call you soon."

Henry hoped he would. He and Edward didn't have many friends, but that was changing, and he liked it. He wouldn't mind one more friend, maybe someone he'd known for a bit longer.

Alcott couldn't say he'd expected this when he'd agreed to

take Edward and Henry to visit their grandfather, but he was happy. He liked that Henry wasn't putting him in the background, treating him only as his bodyguard, that he hadn't hesitated to come out to his grandfather. Of course, part of that clearly had to do with how much Henry disliked his grandfather. He'd wanted to irritate the man, and he'd done exactly that by telling him that he was dating a man, and an air wielder to boot. Alcott didn't think that was the only reason Henry had told his grandfather about him, though. He knew Henry, and he wouldn't be with him only to be a pain in the ass.

He gestured toward the end of the hallway. "If you're ready to go?" he asked.

They needed to get away from the house. Alcott didn't like it. It was too open, with too many places in which people could hide. He wanted to get Henry back to safety. And to do that, he needed him to leave the house. Henry was still talking with Matias, though, and Alcott wished he would hurry up, even though he understood why Henry was checking in on the other man. They'd talked only briefly, but it was obvious Matias wasn't happy with what was happening in the house, and also that he couldn't get away. Henry was a caring man, and he wanted his friends to be okay. It made Alcott love him even more, and he wouldn't have changed his boyfriend for anything in the world.

Even though someone was out there wanting to kill him.

It was still hard to think of Henry as his boyfriend. Alcott had wanted it since he'd fallen in love with Henry, since he'd realized what a good man he was, but he hadn't thought he would get it. They were so different, and not just because Henry was a CEO and Alcott was his bodyguard. They wielded different elements, came from different lives. None of that mattered, though. Now that Alcott had Henry in his life, he wasn't going to give him up easily, even if Henry asked him to. A part of Alcott would always love Henry, and Alcott would have to deal with it if they broke up.

He wasn't planning on doing anything that would push Henry to break up with him.

Henry turned to him, smiling. "Of course. I don't want to be here when Melchior leaves his office. Call me," he repeated, turning back to Matias. "Or Edward, if you're more comfortable with him. It doesn't matter. We'll be expecting your phone call, and if you don't call, *we'll* call *you*."

Matias smiled. "You won't have to. Give me a few days to settle things down, and I'll contact you."

There was nothing else to say, and Bay, Alcott, Edward, and Henry headed to the entrance. Bay and Alcott were careful, even though they were inside the house. They couldn't know where and when Purity would strike, but they knew they would. It was how they worked. First they threatened people. When those people didn't do what they wanted, they attacked. They'd already done it once to Henry and Edward, but Alcott wouldn't be surprised if they did it again. Now that they knew Henry wasn't dead and that Lyle had been taken out of commission, they would have to do something. Trying to force Henry's hand hadn't worked. They'd find another way.

Alcott had to stop thinking about how he felt about being Henry's boyfriend. He had other things to focus on, more important ones. He wouldn't have a boyfriend if he didn't screw his head on right and focus on Henry's safety. That was the most important thing, and he could think about everything else later.

Besides, they could take their time. Their relationship was new, even though they'd been friends for a while, and Alcott had been in love with Henry for just as long. They'd find their way to each other. They'd already started. The situation they were living wasn't exactly perfect, but they'd find a way, just like Edward and Bay had.

Alcott looked at Bay, but Bay wasn't paying attention to him. He'd known Alcott was in love with Henry, but Alcott hadn't told him about them being together until this morning. Edward might have, but as far as Alcott knew, he hadn't found out until this morning, either. He didn't think Henry had called or texted his brother to let him know, and he was relieved. It was selfish, but he'd wanted Henry to himself for a bit, and he'd had him, even if only for one evening. Now they had to focus on everything else—their safety, taking Henry and Edward home, finding out who was pulling the Purity strings.

Alcott wasn't sure why, but he felt like his skin was crawling as if something was about to happen.

He stepped closer to Bay. "Can you feel it too?" he asked, hoping he was imagining it.

Bay's expression was grim when he looked at Alcott. "Yeah. I don't know what it is, though."

"Me neither." But they both had been doing this job for long enough that they knew they should listen to their instincts. It was telling them something was about to happen, and they had to keep that in mind. "In the house?" Alcott asked.

Bay hesitated, then shook his head. "I don't think so. I mean, there are more than enough spots to hide, but I doubt they would attack here. It's too closed up. Edward and Henry know the place, and they could hide. No. If they're going to attack, they'll do it outside, probably on the road."

"We should call Dakota. He can send someone." Although whether they would get there in time was anyone's guess.

Bay nodded curtly. "Do that. We can tell Edward and Henry when we're in the car."

Because Henry and Edward weren't paying attention to Bay and Alcott and what they were saying. They were walking ahead, leaning toward each other, and murmuring.

Alcott didn't want to interrupt the conversation, especially if it was to tell them they suspected Purity was about to attack. They had to know, though. Bay and Alcott might be wrong, but they also might be right, and everyone needed to be prepared.

First, though, Alcott took his phone out. He didn't have to call Dakota to tell him what was going on. A text was more than enough, and he made sure to explain everything, including the fact that he and Bay didn't have any proof they were about to be attacked. Dakota would send someone anyway. He knew what the situation was like, and he would want to make sure the brothers were safe.

Everything was still normal when they stepped out of the house. The car was still there, and while Alcott waited with Edward and Henry, Bay checked it over, just in case. They wouldn't put it past Purity to put a bomb under it or somehow to sabotage it.

But there was nothing, and the four of them climbed into the car. Alcott could feel the tension in the air, and he knew it came from both him and Bay. He also knew the brothers would notice eventually, so he wasn't surprised when as soon as they were settled in, Henry tapped his shoulder.

"What's going on?" he asked. He sounded puzzled, but his voice was steady. He wasn't afraid, not yet.

Alcott and Bay exchanged a glance, and Bay nodded. Alcott looked back at Henry as Bay turned on the car. "We think Purity might be about to attack."

Henry's eyes widened. "How can you know that?"

"It's not a certainty, but it would make sense. It's going to take us a while to get back home. It's an hour's drive, and it would have been easy enough for them to realize where we were going and send someone. We're going to be exposed, in the middle of the road, with no one else around. I already texted Dakota, and he'll send someone, but in the meantime, it's going to be us against them."

"You think they'll take the opportunity because we're alone and isolated."

"It's what they do, and they already know they can't force your hand. They tried, and you ignored them. They need another way to get what they want, and since they don't care about anyone's lives, the best way to do that is to attack you and take you or Edward so they'll have leverage."

Henry nodded and looked out the window. "I see. I hope nothing happens, but . . ."

But it probably would, and they were going to have to face it.

When they stopped the car in the middle of the road, Henry knew what was happening. He peeked through the front window, groaning at the sight of a mound of dirt and a group of men waiting for them. He groaned. "Again?" he asked, even though he'd known to expect it.

Alcott looked at him. "We knew it would happen."

"And we can't, like, drive around them or anything?"

"We can try, but I doubt it will work. They know what kind of element we each wield. They know what to expect from us, and they're probably ready to face us." He turned to Bay, and Bay nodded.

Henry didn't like the way they were looking at each other. He knew they worked together often, but he could see something in their expression, something that told him he wasn't going to like what came next.

Alcott turned to him again, and sure enough, Henry hated the next words that came out of his mouth. "You and Edward need to stay in the car," Alcott said, his tone uncompromising.

It was a good thing Henry wasn't afraid of him or to go

against his wishes. "Why? We can help you."

"You can help us by staying in the car. That way, we won't have to worry about your safety, and we can focus on these guys."

Henry peeked outside again. *These guys*, as Alcott had said, weren't going to just stand there and stare at them. They had precious little time to decide what to do, and they were wasting it. "I've had enough of being attacked."

Alcott shook his head as he reached for the door. "I know that, and I know you're strong enough to face those guys and win. You have to stay with Edward, though. He's still in pain, and he needs you to protect him."

Henry scowled at Alcott. He'd said the exact words he knew would keep Henry where he was. "I hate you," he said.

Alcott smiled at him. "We both know that's a lie. I love you, too, and I'll be careful. I promise."

Henry couldn't do anything else but watch Bay and Alcott climb out of the car and close the doors behind themselves. He wanted to go after them. He wanted to keep them safe, to make sure they would make it out of this alive and in one piece. He needed them to. He'd just found Alcott, and he didn't want his boyfriend to be taken away from him so soon.

He loathed Purity. He despised what they were doing, and he wanted to find out why. If he did, he might have been able to find a way out of the situation. Instead, he had to watch as Bay and Alcott placed themselves in front of the car and faced the group of men waiting for them.

"I think we should help," Edward said.

Henry turned his attention to him. "You're still in pain. You *can't* help."

Edward scowled at him. "I might be in pain, but I can get over it if it means saving Bay. He's my mate, Henry. I have to be there for him. I have to help him."

Henry knew how he felt. He and Alcott might not be mates,

but that didn't mean he didn't want his boyfriend to be safe. "We'll be a hindrance. You heard them. They want us to stay here."

"What if something happens to them?"

Henry looked at the two men again. "Then we'll intervene. Not before, though. I don't think they were wrong when they said they'd be distracted if they knew we were out there. They're not just our bodyguards. They love us, and that will influence what they do." Henry disliked it, but they didn't have a choice. "We'll stay in the car until we can't anymore."

Because if there was one thing he was sure of, it was that he and Edward would have to intervene. Bay and Alcott were good at what they did. They were good fighters, as Henry had seen with his own eyes. There were only two of them, though, while there were eight people to fight against. If Purity did what they'd been doing until now, the men Bay and Alcott would have to fight belonged to different elements. Bay and Alcott wielded water and air, and that would help them. It would be even more useful if they had one more element, and they could if Henry and Edward fought.

Henry had promised, though, so he stayed in the car, watching. He was in awe of the way Alcott wielded his element. He used the slight breeze in the air, reinforcing it, using it to fling people away. He didn't even look where they landed or whether they stood up again. He just threw them this way and that, slamming them around, pushing them away. None of them got to the car, but it couldn't last forever.

Henry sucked in a breath when one of the men finally reached Alcott. He tried to grab Alcott, but Alcott was faster, punching him in the face. When the man stumbled back, Alcott moved forward, punching him again, then kicking his legs to knock them out from under him.

The man dropped like a sack of potatoes, but he tried to get up again. That was when Bay came in. He did something with his element, probably started pulling the water out of the man, and the man started wriggling on the ground, gasping. Bay had to stop, though, when another two men rushed them.

Edward and Henry looked at each other. "It's not going well," Edward murmured.

Henry couldn't deny that. He didn't want to create even more problems for Bay and Alcott, but he also couldn't stay here and watch them being beaten. They'd already taken out two of the people attacking them, but there were still six of them, and they knew what they were doing. One of them, a fire wielder, kept trying to burn both Alcott and Bay, and the only reason he hadn't yet was that Bay was fighting him with his water. Eventually, something would break, though, and Henry could only hope it wouldn't be Bay and Alcott.

"I'll put you in danger if I go," Henry murmured. Because if he left the car, Edward would, too.

"I'll go without you," Edward pointed out. "I love you, Henry, and I love Bay, but neither of you can tell me what to do. Bay needs my help, and I'll give it to him. I'm not going to wait for you to make a decision. I'm going whether you like it or not." And with that, he reached for the door.

Henry looked up just in time to see a man attacking Alcott from behind. He reached out, pushing his power through the windshield, calling to the earth to raise a shield between Alcott and the man. Alcott had noticed him, too, and he'd reached out with his own element, attempting to blast the man away. Instead, his air hit Henry's earth shield, and Henry's eyes widened when instead of destroying each other, they mingled.

He'd never seen that before, but he'd heard about it. Hell, the last person to tell him about it had been his brother, and when he turned to look at Edward, he found Edward staring at him with wide eyes. Then Edward shook his head. "We should have expected it."

"Does that mean what I think it means?" Henry asked.

"Pretty sure it does. Now come on. Let's go get our mates. They need us."

Even though Henry was still stunned at what had just happened, Edward was right. They had to focus on getting their men back and keeping them safe. They might not be bodyguards, but they could use their elements as well as Bay and Alcott did.

Together, they stepped out of the car.

Alcott wished he had more time to watch the union between his element and Henry's.

He had no doubt that was what had happened. He'd been about to be attacked, and Henry had tried to protect him. He'd put up an earth shield, and at the same time, Alcott had used his air to blast away the man who'd been about to hit him. It had worked, and as it did, his air and Henry's earth had mixed. Instead of the earth being blasted away along with the guy, it had mingled with the air, rising above them, mixing until they were one. That could only mean one thing—Alcott and Henry were mates.

It was hard to wrap his mind around it, although Alcott supposed he shouldn't be surprised. He'd never fallen in love so easily or so quickly. Now he knew why. He would have to protect his mate, though. He and Henry would only be able to talk about it if both of them made it out of the attack alive, and Alcott was going to do just that. He couldn't lose Henry, not when he'd just found him, not when they'd just realized they were mates.

So he turned his attention back to the fight.

He was grateful that Henry, and probably Edward, were paying attention. He'd noticed the man about to attack him, and he'd managed to blast him away, but he also might not have, and he'd be dead by now.

Because these people weren't fighting to take him or Bay. They were fighting to kill them. They didn't care about them. They wanted Henry and Edward, and they would mow down their bodyguards if that was what they needed to do.

Alcott blasted an earth wielder who came too close, slamming him against one of the cars parked by the earth mound Purity had raised. He heard the crunch of bones breaking, but he didn't pause to check whether the guy would be able to get to his feet. If he did, Alcott would slam him against something else until he stayed down.

Then a wall of earth rose between him and the fighters again. He turned, not at all surprised to see Henry wasn't in the car anymore. He and Bay had known the brothers wouldn't listen to them, not when it came to this. Henry nodded at him, and they both turned their attention back to the fight.

It was easy now. Bay and Alcott had already gotten rid of several of the fighters, and with Edward and Henry's help, they made quick work of the others. Edward and Henry stayed away, wielding their element from a distance and mostly to protect Bay and Alcott from attacks. It still took work, but soon they were done, and they hadn't even needed the people Dakota had sent. They were nowhere in sight, but they would make a good cleanup team once they arrived.

Alcott looked around, making sure that everyone who needed to be down was. He was panting, and he couldn't wait to take a shower and go to bed, but he stayed attentive and tense. He couldn't relax, not when someone might still be hiding close by. "You see anyone else?" he asked Bay.

Bay had a bleeding gash on his forehead, but apart from that, he looked fine. "I think we got them all. There were eight of them, right?"

Alcott nodded and counted the bodies on the ground.

Some of them were still moving, groaning, holding their limbs. They were hurt, but Alcott didn't feel sorry or guilty. They'd gotten what they deserved. "We got them all. How far away is Dakota? He might be able to use those who are still alive to get more info on Purity."

"We can tie them to the trees. I want to take Edward home, though. I don't think staying here is a good idea, especially not in these circumstances. I want to make sure Purity doesn't send anyone else."

Alcott was tempted to interrogate the people on the ground, but Bay was right. They were bodyguards, and their job was to focus on Edward and Henry. And even if they hadn't been bodyguards, they would need to focus on their mates. They were the most important things, and Alcott wasn't about to fuck things up before he and Henry even had a chance to talk.

He and Bay tied the men to trees. They had to drag a few, and they ignored the screams of pain. Most of them had broken limbs, open gashes that were still bleeding, but Alcott ignored all of that. Once they were done, he turned his attention back to the car.

Henry and Edward were sitting in the backseat, talking to each other. They both looked up when Bay and Alcott came closer, and Henry was out of the car before Alcott could climb in. He threw himself at Alcott, and Alcott caught him, blinking. He hadn't been expecting this kind of reaction, although maybe he should have.

He rubbed his hand up and down Henry's back, trying to soothe him. "I'm fine. I promise."

Henry pushed himself away so they could look at each other. "You're fine, thanks to me."

It made Alcott smile. "I am. Thank you for saving me."

"I couldn't lose my mate as soon as I found him. We're not done, you and I. Far from it."

Alcott agreed. "Let's head home. We can talk there."

Henry looked away. "What about these people?"

"Dakota will take care of them once he gets here. Don't worry about them. They're not going anywhere."

Henry grimaced, but to Alcott's relief, he climbed back into the car. Alcott only relaxed when they were far enough away that the people that they'd left behind wouldn't be able to hurt them. Purity might still have sent someone else, but Alcott doubted it. Even though they seemed to have a lot of people working for them, it had to be hard to recruit element wielders who shared their opinions yet were also willing to work with other elements. There weren't many element wielders in the country. Between the three attacks—the two against Edward and Henry, and the one against Dakota and Benedict—they'd taken out a good number of people who worked for Purity. Alcott wouldn't be surprised if Purity was starting to have numbers problems.

"So, mates," Bay said. The corner of his lips curled into a smile.

Alcott shrugged. He couldn't help but smile himself. "I guess so."

"Can't say it's a surprise."

"It is for me. I didn't expect it."

Bay spared Alcott a glance. "Really? Because it was pretty obvious. I've never seen you fall this hard and fast."

Alcott had been thinking that, too, so Bay wasn't wrong. "It makes sense now."

"I'm happy for you. For *both* of you." Bay paused, his eyes widening. "You do realize that this makes us brothers-in-law, don't you?"

Alcott laughed. "That's not a problem for me. Is it going to be one for you?"

"Hell, no. We've always been brothers. Now, it's official."

And Alcott loved it.

He was relieved when Bay and Edward dropped him and Henry off at Henry's apartment, though. It wasn't just that he and Henry were mates. It was that he wanted to check in on Henry, to make sure he was safe. He wasn't hurt, not physically. He hadn't come close enough to the fight to be. That didn't mean he wasn't in pain, though. He shouldn't have to go through two attacks so close together. Hell, he shouldn't have to go through even one attack, yet here they were, fighting for their lives. It wasn't fair, and Alcott wanted to make sure Henry was okay.

They were silent in the elevator, then again when they got to the apartment. Alcott told Henry to stay where he was. He wouldn't take a chance, so he went in, making sure no one had entered while they were away. Once he was sure the apartment was safe, he came back to the door and opened it wider, waving at Henry to come in.

He turned around, about to ask Henry a question, but the words never left his lips. Henry was on him then, trying to climb him, pushing him against the wall, kissing him.

Alcott had nothing to say to that.

He grabbed Henry's ass and helped him up. He didn't have to explain—Henry jumped, wrapping his legs around Alcott's waist as Alcott stumbled, and they almost crashed to the floor. Henry squeaked, but he was right back on Alcott's mouth again, kissing him as if he were trying to steal the breath out of him. Alcott didn't mind, but he had to know what was going on. Was this just happening because they'd found out they were mates, or was there more to it? He didn't want to only take care of Henry's body. He wanted to take care of his brain, his heart, and his feelings. And to do that, he had to know what was going on in them.

"What is it?" he asked when Henry finally allowed him to breathe.

Henry shook his head and buried his face against Alcott's

neck. He kissed and nipped the skin, and it took all Alcott had to focus on words rather than on what Henry was doing. He pushed Henry against the wall, unwilling to let him go, and reached up to cup one of his cheeks. "What is it?" he repeated.

Henry swallowed, his Adam's apple bobbing up and down. "I want you."

"And I want you, too. But this is a bit . . . sudden."

Henry looked away, and Alcott let him. They might be in love, and they might be mates, but it didn't mean they were entirely comfortable with each other yet. As long as Henry talked to him, Alcott wouldn't mind if he wasn't looking at him as he did so. "I thought I'd lose you."

Alcott understood how Henry felt. "I thought I'd lose you, too. But we're both here. I know it'll be next to impossible to forget what happened, but we should focus on the future, not the past."

Henry snorted. "Purity isn't going anywhere. They're our future."

Alcott shook his head and lightly kissed Henry. "They're not. Eventually we'll get rid of them, and when we do, we'll have our entire lives in front of us. That's what you need to focus on. And I'm not going anywhere. We can have sex if you want, but we can also take our time. We don't have to rush into this because we think we won't have another chance at it."

Henry rolled his eyes and gently slapped the back of Alcott's head. "That's what you think I'm doing? Alcott, I want to have sex with you because I love you, and I think you're sexy. I've wanted to have sex with you since the first time I saw you, even though I was still engaged. It has nothing to do with possibly losing you and everything to do with having blue balls. I know I won't lose you. I'm done waiting, though."

Alcott suspected there was also a good dose of fear behind

this, but Henry was an adult. He knew Alcott would back off if he changed his mind, and Alcott wouldn't stop every five minutes to ask if he was still okay with it, not as long as they talked now. "What do you want, then?"

"Everything you're ready to give me."

"That doesn't tell me a lot. What do you like?" Alcott frowned. Henry was obviously on the rainbow spectrum since he was with him, but that didn't mean he had any kind of experience with men. "Do you know?"

Henry hooked a hand behind Alcott's neck and pulled him closer. "I just told you, I want everything you're ready to give me. You can fuck me, or I can fuck you. We can blow each other, or frot. I'm up for everything, as long as it's with you." He kissed Alcott. "And I have condoms in my bedroom, so you don't have to worry about that."

Alcott pushed away from the wall. "Let's go, then."

Henry laughed, and he sounded better than he had before. It was hard to walk with him wrapped around Alcott's body, but Alcott managed, and he only had to stop three times so they could make out against the wall.

When they finally made it to the bedroom, Alcott dropped Henry onto the bed. Henry laughed, and he looked so good, spread out on the white comforter with his tie askew and his suit jacket all rumpled. Alcott couldn't wait to have him naked, though, and he climbed on top of him, hovering there for a moment before leaning down to kiss him. Henry pushed up, meeting Alcott halfway. Their lips and tongues met, slick and warm and *heaven*.

Alcott moved down to Henry's neck, kissing a trail down, then up to his mouth again. While he kissed Henry, he moved to open Henry's shirt, button by button, revealing skin he couldn't wait to touch. Henry smiled at him and grabbed the bottom of Alcott's shirt, not bothering with buttons and pulling it up so Alcott could slide out of it.

Alcott laughed at Henry being so impatient, and Alcott didn't mind, not now that he knew what was behind it. He finished unbuttoning Henry's shirt and pushed it off his shoulders, then took off the undershirt, too, while Henry tried to do the same with him. They both threw the shirts somewhere to the floor, then they were naked chest against naked chest, and Alcott sighed in pleasure.

They kissed again. Alcott ran his hands down Henry's chest, holding him close with one arm around his back. He kissed down, stopping at Henry's nipple to suck and bite until Henry squirmed under him and tried to push him lower. Henry's cock tented his pants, and while Alcott wanted to go straight to the point, he also didn't want to rush.

He linked their fingers together and went back to kissing Henry, but that didn't last long. Henry pushed his free hand between them and managed to open Alcott's jeans. He grinned against Alcott's mouth, then, to Alcott's surprise, he rolled them so that Alcott was under him.

Alcott watched Henry as he licked down his chest and stomach, then came to hover over Alcott's open jeans. He looked up. His lips were red and slick with their combined saliva. He was still smiling, and he was gorgeous. He wasn't the neat, cool Henry anymore. Under Alcott's hands and his kisses, he looked debauched and happy, which was how Alcott wanted him.

Henry opened the flaps of Alcott's jeans and reached in. He kissed Alcott's stomach just above his cock, focusing on his bellybutton for a moment. Then he finally went down.

He helped Alcott wiggle out of his jeans. They got stuck at Alcott's ankles, and Alcott cursed that he couldn't open his legs wider, but he forgot all about it when Henry's lips closed around his cock. Henry's mouth was warm and welcoming, and Alcott groaned, pressing the back of his head against the pillow.

Henry licked up and down Alcott's cock, looking at him the entire time. Alcott couldn't look away, either. He pressed his lips together and watched as Henry sucked his cock into his mouth. He focused on the head for a while, lavishing it with kisses and licks, then finally sucking until Alcott thought he would go crazy. Henry's fingers felt strong wrapped around the root of Alcott's dick, and Alcott tried to focus on that so he wouldn't come in Henry's mouth as Henry bobbed his head up and down.

"Condoms?" Alcott asked. His voice was rough and growly.

It seemed to delight Henry, who let go of Alcott's cock and straightened. "Nightstand. Grab one and the lube while I get rid of my clothes, would you?"

Alcott could only obey, and while he was able, he finished undressing. When he turned back to the bed, Henry was stretched out on his stomach with his head turned so he could look at Alcott. When he saw Alcott looking back, he opened his legs, making what he wanted obvious. Alcott grinned and climbed between his legs, taking a moment to admire his mate. Henry was the only man he'd have sex with for the rest of his life, and he was surprisingly fine with that.

Alcott opened the condom and rolled it down his cock. His hands trembled, but Henry didn't say anything about it. He just laid there, and when Alcott opened the lube and gently touched a finger to Henry's hole, Henry sighed heavily and lowered his forehead to the bed. He was letting Alcott take care of him, just like Alcott had let Henry take care of him earlier.

Alcott was careful. He didn't know if Henry had ever done this, and he wanted it to be enjoyable for both of them. Once he had Henry pushing back against his fingers and humping the bed, though, he couldn't slow down anymore. He had four fingers in his mate's ass, and he prayed they would be enough.

He straddled Henry's thighs, closing Henry's legs with his, and kissed Henry's shoulder. "Still okay?"

Henry nodded without looking at him. "More than okay, and I'm going to come all over the comforter if you don't get inside me."

Alcott laughed. He moved slightly back and positioned himself, took his cock in hand, and pushed the head against Henry's hole. Henry tensed, and Alcott did his best to soothe him, rubbing his free hand up and down Henry's side as he pushed into him, murmuring things that probably didn't make much sense. It was enough, though, and Henry relaxed as Alcott bottomed out inside him. They both paused for a moment, enjoying the feeling of being one and knowing they would have this for the rest of their lives.

Then Alcott moved. He kept kissing Henry's back, his shoulders, his neck as he fucked him. He rolled his hips, not wanting to push too hard when they were just starting, but that didn't last long. He wanted Henry badly, and his hips snapped as he straightened enough to press his fists against the mattress and use them as leverage to fuck his mate. Henry crossed his ankles, and while it didn't allow for a deep penetration, it was more than enough.

Henry was beautiful spread under Alcott. He arched his back, meeting Alcott thrust for thrust and driving them both crazy. Alcott couldn't touch Henry's cock in this position, though, so he helped Henry to his knees and wrapped himself around him, holding him as close as he could without hindering his movements.

When he reached around Henry, he found his cock damp. Henry sucked in a breath, and Alcott knew he was close. That was okay — he was, too.

Henry shuddered under Alcott as he fucked him with his dick and his hand, moaning as he came. His cock pulsed in

Alcott's hand. Alcott gritted his teeth, wanting Henry to enjoy his orgasm, fucking him through it until Henry slumped. Then, Alcott let go and fucked his mate until he finally came inside him.

He screwed his eyes shut and threw his head back as the pleasure washed over him. Henry stayed still, too, until Alcott was done. Then, he wriggled his ass, making Alcott's eyes pop open. "Are you uncomfortable?" Alcott asked.

Henry shook his head. "I don't think I've ever felt better."

Alcott wished he could stay where he was forever, but he should take care of his mate. He gently withdrew, kissed the middle of Henry's back, then got up to take the condom off and grab a cloth from the bathroom.

Henry rolled to his back before he could head to the bathroom and reached out. "Come back to bed."

"We should clean up."

"We can do that later." Henry paused. "Together."

Alcott couldn't say no to that.

CHAPTER SEVEN

Henry knew it wasn't over by a long shot, but he felt the four of them deserved some time off. He looked around the table, smiling. He, Alcott, Edward, and Bay were having dinner at his apartment. It was a way to reward themselves for coming out of the attack in one piece, but also to spend time together.

Henry felt that he hadn't seen Edward enough lately, and he knew that impression wasn't going to change. He would have to get used to it. He and Edward weren't alone anymore. They weren't each other's everything, and they both had a love beyond their relationship as brothers.

It hadn't been like this with Jessica. Henry had spent a lot of time with her, but Edward had always been there, hovering in the background. He'd been alone then, but he wasn't anymore, and Henry couldn't have been happier for him. Bay was the perfect man for his brother, and he was glad they'd found each other.

He was also glad he and Alcott had found each other.

Sometimes it was still hard to wrap his mind around the fact that they were mates. He'd sworn to himself that he would never attempt to find out if he had another relationship, but that had gone right out the window when Alcott had needed him.

He hadn't hesitated.

He also hadn't expected his element to mix with Alcott's. What were the odds? It was extremely hard for element wielders to find their mates, since the only way they could do that was by mixing their elements, and it wasn't something they did easily. The fact that he and his brother had found their mates over a couple of weeks was incredible, but he wasn't going to look a gift horse in the mouth. He was happy, both for himself and for Edward, and he wanted nothing to change.

Well, except when it came to Purity.

"Has Dakota found out anything from the guys he got from the attack?" he asked.

He realized he'd probably interrupted the conversation when three pairs of eyes turned to look at him. He shrugged, not caring one bit. If he couldn't be himself with these people, who could he be himself with?

Alcott shook his head and reached over the table to take one of Henry's hands. "Most aren't talking, and the ones who are don't know much. Purity is smart. The people in charge are never seen. They give their orders to underlings who then pass them on. The guys who attacked us were at the bottom of the barrel. They don't know who they got the orders from."

"So there's still no way for us to find out who's behind Purity." It was infuriating, and Henry wanted it to change.

He didn't know how, though. They were doing everything they could. Purity, whoever it was, was smart. They knew what they were doing, and they were doing it well. They were hiding, and no one seemed to know who was actually behind the group. From what Henry had seen during the latest attack, he doubted the real motive was element Purity. They wouldn't be using all four elements if that were the case.

That meant they were after something else, and it was too easy to understand what it was. By pushing the elements apart, they were keeping control. They were after power—manipulating the elements—and Henry didn't like it. But there was nothing he could do. No matter how hard he and the others tried, they couldn't find out who was behind

Purity.

Alcott squeezed his hand. "I know you're angry," he started.

Henry snorted, but he squeezed back. "Angry is an understatement. I loathe Purity. They want us to be weak, and eventually, they're going to manage that if we don't stop them."

Alcott shook his head. "We'll only be weak if we allow them to do that to us. It won't be easy, but we can do it. I know we can."

"What if they attack again?" It wasn't an unreasonable fear. Henry didn't just have to worry about Edward anymore. He also had to worry about Alcott, and Bay, and even Dakota and Benedict. He had a whole list of people he cared for who might find themselves in the crossfire, and he had to do something to protect them. What, though? It wasn't his job. His job was to make deals, to earn money, to try to help people, but not this way.

He was relieved when his phone rang. He smiled at the other three, hoping they wouldn't mind. He wanted to answer, even though they were at dinner because he needed a distraction. He knew that once he went back to the table, the conversation would have shifted to something else, and he'd be able to settle down.

His phone was on the kitchen counter, and he answered it without checking the number. "Hello?" he asked.

There was a pause, and the line crackled. Then, a soft voice came through. "Henry? You told me I could call you if I needed you."

It took Henry a moment to realize who was talking. "Matias. I expected you to call sooner." But Henry had been too lost in his own thoughts about the attack, Purity, about finding out Alcott was his mate. Now he felt guilty for not calling Matias himself like he'd threatened he would do. "I'm glad you called, though. What can I do for you?"

"I need help. I'm on the run."

That was the last thing Henry expected to hear, and he knew the others had to hear it, too. "Tell me what's going on," he said as he walked back into the dining room. His tone got everyone's attention, and Alcott rose from his chair, ready to come to him. Henry shook his head and put the phone on speaker, then put it on the table so they could all listen.

"I didn't mean to find this out. I heard a conversation," Matias said.

Now that Henry was listening, he thought Matias was running. From what or whom, Henry didn't know, but he wanted to help.

"A conversation?" Edward asked.

It was a pause, then Matias asked, "Edward?"

Henry had to keep the conversation on the right path. "I put the phone on speaker. Tell us what happened. Tell us what we can do to help."

Matias swallowed loudly. "My mother. She was talking with Melchior. They're the heads of Purity, Henry."

Henry's brain didn't seem to understand the words. "What do you know about Purity?" he asked, realizing it was a stupid question as soon as the words were out.

"Not much. They were talking about it, though, and I know it was important. They were angry because the attack against you went badly. They lost another eight people, and they don't have a lot of people, to begin with. They were planning something." Matias hesitated. "I waited until they were gone, then I went into the office. I grabbed all the documents I could find. I even managed to copy part of the stuff that's on Melchior's computer."

Henry sucked in a breath. "Why would you do that? It's dangerous."

"Because they attacked you. I knew what I was doing. Only they found out, and I had to run. I need help."

"And you'll have it. Don't worry about it. We'll take care of you. Just tell us where you are, and we'll find you." It wasn't only because of what Matias had said.

Henry shouldn't be surprised his grandfather was the head of Purity. It was like him to do something like that. He wanted to hear more of what Matias had to say. More importantly, though, he wanted Matias to be safe. What he'd done, looking through the computer, gathering documents, and listening to that conversation, had put his life in danger. If Melchior got his hands on him, he wouldn't hesitate to kill him, and it wouldn't matter that Matias was his secretary's son.

"Where are you?" Henry asked. Because they were sending someone to get him, and they were doing it now. Matias would be safe.

He had to be.

You may also enjoy the following from eXtasy Books Inc:

Lost and Found
Catherine Lievens

Excerpt

Owen was on the edge of panic by the time the car stopped. He couldn't go back, but he was terrified of going forward.

He shouldn't be. Toby had been nothing but kind to him, and even though his mate, the Rosewood alpha, and the other man in the car hadn't spoken much, Owen didn't feel threatened by them.

He could be wrong. He'd been before. But he didn't feel like they were a threat to him, and he hoped he wasn't wrong. He wanted this to work, even though it was crazy. He wanted the Rosewood pack to be his new home, and he prayed that was what would happen. He would have to get over his fear, though, and he wasn't sure he could.

He knew his eyes were wide as he climbed out of the car. For some reason, he wanted to get back inside. He'd felt calmer there, maybe because he already knew Toby, even though he didn't know him well. He'd felt comfortable, excited, and wary, but now, he was in the open, and he didn't know what to do.

Two men rushed closer as soon as they saw them. One of them almost tumbled off the steps when he came down the porch, but the other held him up, and they moved toward their group. Owen held his breath, but they ignored him, instead fussing over Toby. One of them looked so much like Toby that Owen didn't have a doubt they were related. He didn't know who the other one was, but they were obviously good friends, and it made Owen both envious and hopeful.

Maybe he could have this, too. He never really had a friend. Even when he'd been a child, most of the other wolf shifters in the pack had avoided him. He didn't understand why, although he suspected it had to do with his father, or maybe because Owen was forbidden to shift. For whatever reason, his wolf was a monster, or at least, it was what Owen believed. Maybe the other wolf shifters could feel it. Maybe the shifters in Rosewood would feel it, too, and they would tell him they'd been wrong, that they couldn't take him in.

He swallowed. He had to keep his mind off that. He couldn't show the Rosewood pack he was afraid or that he wasn't normal, not yet. Maybe later if they accepted him. But right now, he had too much to lose.

He looked around. The pack looked very much like the Springfield pack had. They were both in the middle of the forest, with houses scattered around a small clearing. People were peeking from the windows, sitting on the porch, kids playing around, some in their wolf form, others in their human form. It felt like home, even though it wasn't, and it helped Owen relax.

Not entirely, though. He made sure to stay away from Toby and his friends, but he found himself at a loss. Camden, his new alpha, was talking to someone, possibly his beta. One of the twins was talking to another man, and from the way they leaned toward each other, he suspected the man was his mate, or someone just as important. That left Owen on his own, or rather, it left him with the man who had ridden with him, Toby, and Camden.

They hadn't been introduced, and they hadn't even talked, but Owen knew him more than he knew the people peering at him from their windows, so he moved closer. Even if the guy decided he wanted nothing to do with Owen, Owen doubted he would say anything to his face.

The wind played with the man's long blond braid, and Owen wished he had enough courage to ask him for his name. He moved even closer and forced himself to smile.

That was when he smelled it.

He looked around for a moment, wondering where the smell was coming from. He'd never smelled anything like that, and he'd never felt this way about anything. He knew what it was. All shifter children were taught how to recognize their mate, and he knew that was who he was smelling.

Owen's mate was a member of the Rosewood pack.

He felt his knees buckle, but he managed to stay on his feet as he continued looking around. From where the wind was coming, it wasn't hard to guess who his mate was, and he couldn't believe he hadn't realized it before. He'd been riding with his mate next to him in the car. How had he not smelled him?

Owen looked at his mate. Maybe his mate hadn't realized, either, and that was why he hadn't said anything. Or maybe he had realized, but he'd given Owen space. He might also not want Owen. Maybe Owen wasn't his type.

Owen didn't know what to think, but he had to stop freaking out before he had a panic attack. His mate hadn't said anything to him, so he shouldn't assume his mate didn't want him. Maybe he truly hadn't smelled Owen. The car windows had been open after all, and there had been another two people in the car with them.

He moved toward his mate, ready to ask for his name, but that moment, Camden stepped toward him. Owen forced himself to stop and looked at his new alpha.

"How are you feeling?" Camden asked.

Owen forced himself to smile. "Fine. Confused and

bewildered, but I'll be okay."

Camden nodded. "That's normal. But if you're not sure you're okay, I can call our healer."

"I'll be fine. It's just a lot to process."

"I understand. You're shaken. You don't have to worry about anything, though. I don't know what your story with the Springfield pack is beyond what you told us in the car, but you don't ever have to go back if you don't want to. Alpha Johnson was clear about that. As long as you want to live here, you're a member of the Rosewood pack."

Owen didn't know what to say to that, except, "Thank you."

"You have nothing to thank me for. If anything, I should be the one thanking you. You helped my mate when he needed it, and I'm more than happy to welcome you in my pack. You can stay in one of the guest rooms in our house."

"I don't want to be a bother."

"You won't be. You're not the only one staying with us right now. Lennox is, too."

Owen looked around, trying to understand who Lennox was, and Camden pointed at his mate.

"That's Lennox," he explained. "He and his twin Carey are phoenix shifters, and I asked them to come here to protect my mate and his brother. They did a good job. Carey moved out since he met his mate, and both of them and their boyfriend are living together. Lennox is still with us, though, and I hope that won't be a problem for you. He won't hurt you."

Owen looked away from Lennox. He had a name now, and he wanted to step closer, to talk to him. There had to be a reason Lennox hadn't talked to him yet, though.

Their gaze crossed, and for once, Owen didn't look away. He'd been taught all his life not to look up at people, to avoid confrontation, to stay away. His first instinct was to do just that even now, but it was different. Lennox was different. He wasn't just a shifter. He was Owen's mate, and that had to mean something.

"Lennox?" Camden asked, confusion obvious in his voice.

Lennox stepped closer and cleared his throat. "We're mates," he said, his voice rough as if he didn't use it often.

Camden blinked at him. "Really?"

Lennox nodded once, curtly. "Really. I realized in the car, while I think Owen only found out now."

"Well, congratulations."

"Thank you," Owen managed to say.

Camden looked around, and when Toby came closer, he opened his arms to him. He kissed the top of his head, and Owen's heart ached to have the same. He didn't know if he could, but this was his best chance. Lennox was his best chance.

"You can come inside the house if you want, but if you'd rather stay out here and talk with Lennox, you can do that, too," Camden said. "You're a member of the pack, and you can go anywhere you want. Obviously, don't go inside people's houses without knocking and without authorization, but if you want to explore, feel free to do it. Or if you want to come inside the house and take some time to yourself to gather your thoughts, you can do that, too. Pick whatever guestroom you want to stay in."

It was overwhelming. Owen had gone from having only John, who avoided talking to him on the best of days, to living with Toby and Camden — and Lennox. He didn't know what to do with that, but he would have to find a way to deal with it.

About the Author

Catherine is the creator of several series, most of them paranormal, including the Whitedell Pride Series and the Gillham Pack Series. While she graduated in translation, she decided to go the writer's way because it was more fun to create her own stories and characters.

She's been living in Italy for more than twenty years, but she's a daughter of the North — Belgium to be precise — and she misses it so much that she's already planning to move back.

She loves pizza — probably too much — her son, her pets, and of course, books. She sneaks some reading time into her schedule every time she has five minutes free from writing, demands from her various pets and son, and lastly, housework.

Connect with her:

lievens.catherine@gmail.com
BookBub: https://www.bookbub.com/authors/catherine-lievens
Website: https://authorcatherinelievens.com/
Facebook: https://www.facebook.com/catherine.lievens.9
Facebook Group: https://www.facebook.com/groups/411788002341528/
Twitter: https://twitter.com/authorCLievens
Newsletter: http://eepurl.com/c-uvKn

www.ingramcontent.com/pod-product-compliance
Lightning Source LLC
Chambersburg PA
CBHW060629130626
46555CB00002B/720